# Kelsey and King:
# I Used to Love Him

By: Kayla André

## Dedication

For squad! I love y'all and I am so proud of each and every one of you all. Ariyan, Kelsey, Markia, Big Jeraund, and Jonnessia. I truly believe God has brought us together for a reason. You all have helped me during my darkest times and have always been supportive of my writing. This here, it's for you!

# One

**Kelsey**

Back and forth, back and forth I paced in the living room waiting for King to make his way through the doors of our home. He'd been out all night, it was two in the morning and I growing sick of trying to figure out where the fuck he was and why he wasn't in our marital bed.

*"Marry a rapper, it will be fun!"* I mocked my friends as I continued to make dents in my marble floors. I picked up my glass of red wine and took another sip, trying to calm my nerves, but it wasn't helping.

This was starting to tug at my mind. I was a good ass woman and I knew that any nigga would be lucky to have me. I'm a lawyer at one of the top law firms in the city of Atlanta and I was also very submissive to my husband, yet in still King stayed in the streets with any and every bitch with a waist trainer in their closet.

I knew that I needed to be up in five hours to get my daughter to school and get ready for work so I brought my ass upstairs to my bed after I stopped my Kemarr's room to make sure she was still sound asleep.

As I pulled back the sheets to custom bed to accommodate my husband's six-eight/ three-hundred fifty-pound body, I got on my side and snuggled with my favorite pillow and stared at the wedding picture that rested on my nightstand.

The girl on that picture was more than in love. She was excited about what life would bring her and her soulmate. I wish I could go back and tell that innocent girl that those long nights of passionate love making would quickly turn into sleepless nights with a tear stained pillow.

I felt my eyelids get heavy and I knew it was time for me to finally turn in for the night. I couldn't drive around and bring him home. He'd have to show up on his own.

*****

"Kelsey you don't hear me fucking talking to you?" King screamed from the doorway of the kitchen as I placed the hard soled Mary Jane shoes on my four-year old's feet while she sat on the island. "I asked you a question. My momma wants to know what we are doing for Marri's birthday."

I had nothing to say to King. When I felt him come into the bed, it was at six in the fucking morning and his ass wasn't sleepy because he turned on the television. Yet when my alarm went off, he started to snore. Nigga please.

I shot King a look to let him know that he needed to cut that shit out in front of my child. She didn't need to know what all her parents had going all. All she needed to worry about was the fact that her birthday was coming up and that she was about to be going to *big girl* school.

Once Kemarr's shoes were firmly on her feet, I took her off of the counter and placed her on her feet before handing her a juice and her backpack. I grabbed my brief case just as King spoke again. "Come here Daddy baby," King called out to her.

Of course her face lit up at his words and she ran to her father. When he picked her up I couldn't deny the warming sensation I felt. She was an exact replica of her father and he knew it. From his light skin with red undertones to her naturally sleepy eyes.

"Marri you see how your mommy is being mean to me?" He asked her as he smiled at her and then looked at me. See it was little petty shit like this that he did that aggravated me.

"King, give me my child please or we will be late." I looked at the clock on the stove and saw it was eight-thirty. Which meant I only had ninety minutes to get to my office in time for my meeting.

I reached my hands out to get my child, but King turned her away from me as if it was a game. "Why aren't you talking to me?" He questioned. Still holding my child.

"King, don't act like you don't know." I sat my brief case on the island, prepared to play his little game. "What time did you get home?" Placing my hands on my hips I titled my head to the side and rolled my eyes.

King wasted no time giving me back my child. I knew he wasn't willing to have that conversation. "Here the fuck you go with that shit. You always think a nigga cheating on you. Here, take her. I was in the fucking studio."

Kemarr came to me still confused, but she knew not to say anything while mommy and daddy tossed mean words to each other. "You gonna stop acting a fucking ass in front of my child. I swear to god you are." I picked up my brief case and pushed past him.

Reaching the foyer, I placed Kemarr down on her feet and grabbed my phone and keys from the table. King stood in the door way and watched me leave out the door. "Daddy loves you Marri," I heard him scream as I slammed the door.

"I love you too Daddy," Kemarr smiled as continued drinking her juice. I held her hand as we walked down the steps of our home and on to the horseshoe driveway where my Black Escalade sat in front King's matte white Maybach.

I unlocked the doors and held Kemarr's door open for her to get in. I was so happy she was at the age where she was able to buckle herself in. It made everything go so much faster. Getting in myself, I was ready to leave out the gates of my estate and get to work. I was just happy that King and I didn't get into a fight this morning. Today would be a good day!

# Two

## Kelsey

"And what time did he get home last night?" My best friend, Harmonie, sat across from me with an annoyed look on her face. She knew the issues I faced with King and she hated, but she supported whatever decision I made.

I took a sip of my margarita, trying to decide if I was going to give her a real answer or come up with some sort of lie. I mean the only reason she even knew was because when she called me at midnight to tell me about the toe curling head that she'd just received from her little boo thang,

"Around six," I decided to go with the truth. "And got in the bed like nothing was even wrong, He claimed to be at the studio, but you know like I know he was somewhere balls deep inside some chicken head.

Harmonie took her glass to her mouth and rolled her eyes. "Kels, you know whatever the fuck you do, I'd be cool, but you deserve better than this shit. I mean I know I encouraged you to date him, but now I want you to leave. King ain't shit."

She was right, I need to leave, but my mother always told me that divorce wasn't an option. I was willing to put everything I had into my marriage just so I knew that sin wouldn't be counted against me. "Yea I know, but look. I am going to head back to work and wrap up some paperwork so that I can get Kemarr by three-thirty. Her school is now charging a thirty dollar per minute fee if you are late."

Girl I took another sip of my glass before digging my manicured hands into my little Michael Kors clutch to pull out a fifty-dollar bill. I threw it on the table and stood up. "It's on me today," I gave her a kiss on the cheek and left.

I rushed out of the restaurant before my best friend tried to stop me. Unlocking the doors of my truck I heard someone call my name. "Kelsey wait!" I sat down in my truck and looked back trying to see who was calling me.

"Emilio? Emilio Gustavo?" I squinted my eyes trying to make sure that it was him. As he got closer, the smile on his face let me know that I had gotten it right. Emilio's fine ass was my first love. We met while I attended NYU. He stood ay six-foot five and was pure muscle, just like my husband, but unlike King, he was Italian.

"Hey mi Regina, I can't believe that it's you. I haven't seen you in about six years." He opened his arms to give me a hug. I took in his manly scent and almost forgot that I was a married lady.

After Emilio let me go we stared at each other for a few seconds before I broke the ice. "So how have you been? You still…." I turned my lip up, asking him if he was still in the streets. That was the reason why he and I weren't together now. He told me that with the life he lived, he knew that he couldn't have a wife.

"No, no. You are looking at the owner of Louts Casinos and Resorts," he popped the collar of his suit which I'm pretty sure was custom. I held my chest, shocked. Louts was sweeping the nation by storm. It had opened four locations in two years. Hell they were becoming bigger than Margaritaville.

Emilio laughed at my shock. "Well I am so proud of you Milo!" I clapped my hands together. I looked at the clock and noticed that it was getting late. "It was nice seeing you though Milo, but look I have to get back to the office."

He nodded his head, "I am not letting you leave and I don't have your number." He held out his already opened iPhone for me to punch in my numbers.

"You know I am married right?" I held up my fifteen carried wedding ring for him to see. He knew what he was doing, but I just wanted to make sure that he knew that I wasn't trying to go that particular route with him.

"Yea, I was told." He still had his hand out for me to grab his phone. I should my head and obliged to his request and typed in my number, then handed it back to him.

He looked at it and saved it before he placed it back into his pocket. "Alright, I really got to go now." I placed my seat belt over my body and waited for him to move.

"Ok. Nice seeing you. I will be calling," he waved and stepped back into the middle of the street, allowing me to close my door. I smiled at him through the window and started my car and pulled out of my parking spot.

A smile had made its way on to my face and I blushed at the thought of Emilio. I began to wonder what would happen if I had decided not to leave and had stayed with him. I probably wouldn't have been going through half of the bullshit as I do now.

Milo was a powerful ass nigga and he knew it, so he didn't tolerate bullshit. I never had to worry about him with any other females because hell he didn't have the time to cheat. We were only even able to have sex about once a week. He was traveling all across the world to handle shit with different connects and distributors, but when he did come home and we were able to have our time, he pleased himself by pleasing me.

I stopped at my sectary's desk on the way to my office to see if I had any missed calls and of course I did. Growing up it was my dream to become an attorney, a criminal attorney. After my father almost had to serve life in prison for King Pin charges, I knew I wanted to help people with families get off.

I took off my red bottom stilettos as soon as I closed the doors to my corner office. Hell I loved being cute, but I'd much rather be comfortable. My feet got happy as soon as they were freed from their cages and placed on to the red carpeted floors of my office.

Taking a seat at my desk I looked through the message slips that Sharmane, my secretary, had placed in my hands just moments ago. All of these messages didn't require a response, but one. Kemarr's school had called so immediately I returned their call.

"Littles Blessings Academy, how may I direct your call?" The receptionist answered on the second ring.

"Hi, this is Kelsey Taylor, Kemarr Taylor's mother. I missed a call from you all?" I sat up in my seat, praying that nothing bad has happened. She paused for a moment before she told me she was going to transfer my call. I knew something had to be serious in order for me to have to be transferred.

"Mrs. Taylor, this is head mistress Dr. Lovely. I was calling you about an incident we had earlier in regards to Kemarr." She paused and waited for my reply saying that I was listening. Hell she was dragging the story on too long.

"Yes ma'am. I am listening." I bit my bottom lip. The things going through my mind were crazy. I also was wondering why the fuck they were prolonging the story.

She took a deep breath before she continued with the story. "Lately Kemarr has been having a few problems controlling her anger and today she actually got into a fist fight with a male student in her class."

As soon as she told me what happened, I knew I couldn't blame anymore, but King and myself. Hell all the arguing we had been doing, Kemarr was watching us and she was unfortunately taking notes. "Mrs. Taylor are you there?"

I nodded my head before my mouth moved, like she could actually see me. "Yes ma'am I am. I am so sorry. Her father and I will talk to her about this. I mean she is only four so we are going to do as much as we can."

"That is fine, but you know here at Little Blessings we have a very strict no fighting policy so Kemarr has been suspended for the rest of the week. She has to be picked up immediately." Her voice became firm as she spoke into the phone.

One-fifteen is what my clock read. *Shit,* I had a meeting with my boss in fifteen minutes. What the fuck was I supposed to do. "Yes ma'am. Let me call her father." I hung up the phone fore Dr. Lovely had a chance to reply. I quickly picked it up and dialed my husband's number, pressing nine first.

*"Hey you've reached Yung Kane. I can't answer my phone right now, but if you need me immediately call my manager or my wife \*beep\*,"* I listened to the bullshit ass message that he had on his voicemail. Yea, maybe when we first got married I would have been able to locate him wherever he was, but as of now he could be out the country for all I know.

"King, I need you to call me back now. It's concerning Kemarr." I huffed, deciding to leave a message, hoping that he would have the decency to call me back.

After waiting three minutes and he still hadn't called, I had to call my boss and ask to reschedule my meeting. "It's fine Kelsey. I understand my mother was a single mother. I wanted to talk to you about this new case. A man has been arrested on King Pin charges. You know there isn't anyone else I trust with this case. I'll leave the folder with your secretary before I leave."

The news made my panties wet. King Pin charges were the hardest charges to fight, but I knew that God would allow me to win. "Yes Sir, Mr. Michelson. I thank you for this opportunity."

"No problem Kels. Just make sure you win this. We haven't lost a case in three years, don't

drop the ball." He laughed, but I knew he was serious. I thanked him again and told him that I had to leave.

I grabbed my belongings and slipped my shoes back on headed out the door, letting my secretary know that she would be receiving a folder for a new case and she needed to get everything ready for me by tomorrow morning and set up a meeting with the client for ten a.m. tomorrow morning.

The interstate wasn't as packed as I thought it would be so I was able to reach Kemarr's school in no time. I checked my phone before exiting my car and still I had no call from my husband and forty-five minutes had passed since I'd called him.

As soon as I stepped into the office, the receptionist left her desk and headed into Dr. Lovely's office. A few seconds later, Kemarr came out of the office with Dr. Lovely with her head down. She looked so cute with her smooth caramel skin and wavy hair that I had placed into a bun that morning with a bow; her baby hairs still neatly rested on her forehead.

"I am so sorry. I promise that this will never happen again," I took my child's hand. Dr. Lovely gave me a side eye, but she didn't open her mouth. "Do I have to sign her out?"

"No, but here are her suspension papers." The receptionist handed me a packed of about four papers. How the fuck does a four-year-old have a stack of papers for a fucking suspension from a daycare?

I took the papers and gave them a slight smile before I turned and walked out the door. My mind was still on the fact that King has yet to call me to check on his child. What if something was actually fucking wrong?

"Am I trouble?" Kemarr was smart for her age. Although her sentence wasn't as proper as yours and mine, she knew what she was talking about. I nodded my head and placed her in her seat. She buckled herself in and started to cry.

I took a deep breath and prepared to parent. "Kemarr, I don't care about your tears you are supposed to keep your hands to yourself, and if someone hits you first, go tell the teacher." I spoke to her in a calm voice. "Do you understand what Mommy is saying?"

She nodded her head and used the back of her hands to wipe her wet face. I hated to see my baby cry, but I couldn't act soft. As she settled down, I closed her door and walked to my door. I looked down at my phone and saw that King had still not called me back. What the fuck was he doing?

# Three

## King

"Ayo Kane, this shit fire yea." My producer took a pull of the blunt before handing it to me. "I feel another Grammy nomination." He rubbed his hands together.

I nodded my head and brought the blunt to my lips for me to hit it. My new shit was hot. The beat was banging and the chorus was catchy. Not to mention I had gotten August Alsina to do the chorus and I was ready for the shit to take over the radio stations.

We continued to listen to the track as we relaxed, enjoying our high. My dick jumped when Leilani walked through the doors of the studio in these tight ass stretchy tie-dye pants and a matching top that looked more like a bra. The bitch was bad. Body like Nicki, but her thighs matched the size her ass. Hair down her back, fuck I ain't care if it was hers or not, the shit did something to me.

"Hello Fellas," she greeted the entire room before she smiled at me. I nodded my head and bit my bottom lip as she made her way over to the sofa I was sitting on and took a seat right next to me. A little too close to say I was a married man.

I scratched my head before I spoke up. "Say, Dee give us a minute please." I nodded my head towards the door. Dee caught my hint and turned off the music before he excused himself and said he'd holla at me later.

Once the door was closed to the sound proof studio I turned my body to face Leilani's fine ass. "So what's up with you Ma?" I licked my lips and I looked at how her nipples were showing through her top.

"I'm good Kane. I came to see my baby since I'm fresh from tour. You know I missed you." Lani scooted closer to me and leaned over to kiss my lips. Even the smell of her perfume turned me on.

I had been seeing Lani since she came into the industry about six months ago when she took the world by storm with her song "Severely". She knew I was married, but she didn't care. Hell me cheating didn't mean I didn't love Kelsey. In fact, I loved her more than I loved myself.

My father always taught me that a man was supposed to have a woman to take care of him sexually and a woman to take care of him mentally, spiritually, and emotionally. Sex was how a man was supposed to get rid of stress so he wouldn't flash out and go mad.

He taught me to never let go of my wife. No matter how hard it was or how good the pussy was in the streets, always go home. A man was supposed to be the bread winner and lead the household, and Kelsey didn't let me be that. She wanted to make her own money and do everything equally, and there is where our problem lied.

"Oh you missed me? Show me," I spread my legs open a little and leaned back into the sofa. Lani was a beast when it came down to giving a nigga some top. She was able to suck peanut butter through a coffee stirrer.

Lani leaned over and took her hands to unbuckle my pants. Once she got my zipper down, she
reached her hands inside of my boxers and pulled my big nigga out. I wasn't front, but I was working with a whopper. Ten inches long and damn near four inches in diameter. Shit as tall and stocky as I am, I had better be working with something.

When she took me into her mouth, I had to bite my lip until it almost bled so I wouldn't bust. Kelsey was so mad at me that she hadn't touched me in about three days and the other bitch I was fucking wasn't as tight as I would have liked her to be, but she stays wet.

Leilani bobbled her head up and down like a see-saw on my dick. She started to message my balls as she continued to do everything in her power to please me. She knew what the fuck to do to make me go crazy. As soon as she took her tongue and licked the tip of my dick I felt my shit start to ooze in her mouth. She placed my dick further down her throat, and swallowed the shit. I released my seeds and allowed them to swim down her throat.

"Get up and bust that shit open," stood up and watched her pull down her pants as she got up and turned around and bent over using her hands to make my entrance easier. Damn her shit was tight.

***

"Where the fuck have you been?" Kelsey greeted me at the door as soon as I opened it with my key. I looked to the left wall and got reminded of the security system that I had installed to keep my family safe. She probably saw my ass coming down the street.

I knew Kelsey was about to be ready to fight, but I was tired as fuck and after I left Leilani, Dee and I hit up the bar for some drinks. "Kelsey, I'm not for the bullshit at all tonight. You need to learn how to welcome your husband home from a long day of making shit happen to provide you with the shit you have."

"Bitch what the fuck are you talking about? Nigga I make damn near two-hundred thousand dollars a year. I can leave you and still be able to live like I am, but your ass has been out all damn day?"

See here the shit started. Kelsey always wanted to remind a nigga how much she fucking made as if I actually gave a fuck. I mean hell I made way more than two-hundred stacks a year, so that shit she was talking about was chump change.

"And why the fuck didn't you bother to call me back, after I left a voicemail telling you that Kemarr was in trouble?" Her words caught me off guard. Kemarr Marie was my entire world and there was no way I would just ignore a message concerning her. My phone was off, but that was because I was so focused on my music I didn't worry about it. I knew that if Kelsey really needed me, she knew how to find me.

"What's wrong with her?" I followed behind my wife as she walked up the stairs to our bedroom, stopping by Kemarr's room first to check on her.

 She was quiet until we got into our room and I closed the door behind us. "Your daughter got into a fight with a male student. All the fighting we are doing is now starting to affect her. She's been suspended from school. The papers have documented three separate incidences of Kemarr cursing."
She tossed the papers at me.

I picked the papers from the floor and looked over them. Apparently my child had told her teacher to kiss her ass; told another child to fuck off, and hit a little boy for *playing with her*. I laughed to myself because I always knew she was a little firecracker like her mother and myself.

"You think that shit is funny? So funny that you have to watch her the rest of the week; I have a new case." Kelsey walked into the bathroom and started to undress to get into the shower.

Mesmerized by my wife's beauty, I couldn't respond right away. She was thick, but not fat. Not a roll on her body, but baby girl was healthy. Just the right amount of ass, but her titties covered my face when she rode me during sex. Her caramel skin always had a glow to it as if she diamonds buried within her. Her short bob emphasized her neck its perfect structure. Kelsey stood tall enough for me not to smash her, but short enough where I had to bend down to kiss her. She was my living Barbie.

"What," I asked, snapping back into reality when I heard the shower water turn on. I walked into the bathroom and stood by the sink and watched her make sure the temperature with her hand, then adjusting it to make it even hotter.

She looked back at me and repeated herself, "You have to watch Kemarr since she's been suspended."

When she turned to walk into the glass shower, I saw the only tattoo she had on her body which was located on the left side of her lower back. When we'd gotten married we'd decided to go get matching tattoos. It was of the king and queen chess pieces. She thought it was cheesy at first, but I thought it was hot as fuck.

"I can't watch her I purchased studio time for all this week." I smacked my lips. I started to argue with Kelsey, but I knew damn well I was already in the dog house and I needed to work my way in her good graces again. "Never mind, she can just learn the music business I guess."

Kelsey laughed to herself, but I didn't even bother to ask her what was so funny because I knew I wasn't going to like her answer and it would lead to a fight. I took my ass into the bedroom to wait for her to get out of the shower. I sat down on her side the bed which was the closest to the bathroom and went through my phone. Leilani had hit me up asking me if I would be able to meet her at some club tonight, but I deleted her thread. She knew better than to hit my line when I was with my family.

Fifteen minutes later my wife walked out of the bathroom wrapped in an aqua colored towel and completely ignored me as she reached on the nightstand and grabbed the bottle of Dove body lotion. I bit my lip in anticipation of what I knew would happen in a few minutes.

As she lifted her leg on the bed and dropped the towel to the floor, my dick jumped. I watched as she squeezed some of the lotion into her hand and massaged into on to her leg. When she moved on to the other leg, which was my cue to get behind her.

"King what are you doing," Kelsey spoke just above a whisper. I didn't reply, I just took my hands and started to massage her shoulders. I knew what it took for my wife to relax and it was my job
as her husband to fulfill that need. "King,"

"Baby, just let me apologize to you. Lay down." I turned her around and she rolled her eyes, but she knew what was coming so she laid down.

"I'm not fucking you so don't take your dick out," Kelsey lifted her head up to warn me. I mean I cleaned myself off, but if she didn't want the dick tonight, then that's cool too.

Nodding my head, I let her know that I understood, but I got down on my knees in front of her and started to kiss on her thick thigs. A slight moan escaped her lips and that made me move to her second pair of lips. I rested her legs on my shoulders and used my hands to open her up as I flicked my tongue up and down on her clit.

Sucking it into my mouth I continued to flick my tongue against her flesh. The moans that were coming from my wife's lips let me know that she needed. I took two fingers and started to push them in and out of her, tickling her g-spot. I felt her walls tighten so I removed my fingers and replaced them with my tongue. Around and around I licked her insides and I circled her clit with my fingers.

Kelsey tasted like pure heaven to me. Although she technically didn't have a taste, when her cum hit my tongue I could always taste a little hint of sweetness. I took my free hand and reached up to message her nipples. Her body started jerking left and right as she climbed towards her climax.

She grabbed the back of my head, shoving my face into her vagina as I ran my tongue from the top of her vagina to the crack of her ass, and back up. "Shit King, you better eat this shit like you know I got the best in the world."

My wife was panting and I knew she was about to squirt so I brought her clit back in my mouth and used my fingers as if they were a penis. "You do Baby," I replied, looking up at the fact that Kelsey was now sitting up.

I started moving my fingers faster and I felt myself being locked into position by Kelsey's thighs. I sucked even hard. "Shit Kane!" She released all her fluids and it shot out right on my hand, soaking up the top of my shirt.

Her body flew back down on the bed and she released me from her hold. "Your shit is so good Kelsey," I kissed her thighs before I stood up to kiss her.

She didn't respond since she was trying to catch her breath. I scooted her up in my arms and pulled back the black comforter and laid my wife down on the bed because she was my queen and I knew she was tired and I knew she was going to go to sleep after the head she'd just received.

Just as I was bringing the comforter back over her body, Kelsey spoke. "You keep fucking those dirty bitches in the streets and you won't even know what my shit smells like let alone how it taste."

Rolling her eyes at me, she turned over and went to sleep, leaving me standing there not knowing what to say. "Goodnight Baby," I bent down and gave her a kiss on her head.

Something was going to have to give because I can't lose my wife, but the constant pussy being
thrown at me was hard to turn down.

# Four

## Kelsey

"Mrs. Taylor your client is already in your office waiting for you." Sharmane greeted me with a caramel and white mocha latte and the case folder. I thanked her and took the coffee from her hand.

I was rushing this morning and didn't have time to get my own coffee. King was acting as if he didn't know what all it took to take care of his daughter for the day. I had to pick out clothes, pack snacks, make sure her iPad was charged, and even wake her up to comb her hair.

Now usually I would have to do her hair and dress her, but I would comb her hair and iron her uniform the night before. Then my husband waited until I was damn near out of the door before he told me he didn't know how to do any of it. I mean he was trying to be nice this morning, waking me up to head, but he blew my orgasmic high by being dumb.

"I am so sorry I'm late," I excused my tardiness as soon as I opened the door to my office. I never looked over at my client as I closed the door, trying not drop all of the things in my arms.

I heard a slight laugh coming from whoever it was in the chair. When I finally turned around I damn near dropped everything. "Emilio, I know you lying."

Milo stood up from the chair in front of my desk and came to help me with the things in my arm and bring them over to my glass desk. Once we got everything settled, Milo started laughing again. "When I asked for the best attorney in Atlanta, I never thought of you."

I really felt offended by his words. The first person that came to his mind should have been me. "No, not like that. That probably came out wrong," He tried his hardest to take back the words that he'd already spoke into the atmosphere.

Nodding my head, I just took a seat behind my desk and opened his file and reviewed it. He was being accused of smuggling 652 kilos of coke across the border and for money laundering. They were saying that his casino was just a big front for his multibillion dollar drug business. If it was proven that he had purchased the casino with drug money, he could lose it.

"Milo, I thought you said you were done with the streets?" I started the conversation as I continued to browse through his case folder. His file was thick as fuck which meant that Milo had been being watched for a while now.

"Kelsey, I promise you I have. This is just some old shit. A girl I was messing with tried to get me into some trouble when I told her I didn't want to talk to her anymore." He leaned forward in his chair, trying to convince me of his story. He could be lying or he could he be telling the truth, but either way my job was to prove that the allegations against him were completely false.

For an entire ninety minutes Emilio and I went over the facts of his case. Page by page, word by word. I wanted him to know that what he was facing was very serious and that he could be facing having to spend the rest of his life behind bars if we didn't win the case. He needed to tell me any and everything that would help me get him off.

After we ran through everything and Emilio told me everything that he thought I needed to know, I came up with a plan on how I was going to get him off without this shit going to trial. When he left, he asked me out to lunch and I accepted.

Yes, I knew a married lady shouldn't be going to have lunch with a man who wasn't her husband, but hell food was food. One thing about it and two things for sure, Kelsey Taylor was not going to turn down free food.

"So how does it feel to be married to the biggest rapper right now? What Yung Kane got like three songs on the radio and he's featured on songs with Rhianna, Future, and DJ Khaled?" Emilio thought he was slick bringing up my husband, but hell it was what it was.

Taking a glance around the home-style restaurant, I began to think about King and the times he and I would spend in restaurants talking long after the waiter had picked up our plates. The love I felt for King was something like electricity in my soul, but I didn't know if he felt the same way about me and it was killing me.

"It's nice, I must admit. The problem is that I have to share my husband with the world. Everyone knows about us, or at least they think they know." I picked up my wine glass and took a sip of it before placing it back down.

Emilio's skin was so beautiful. It was crisp tan, but not too much where he looked too red or too orange, but it was just right. I loved how his hair was kind of hawked in the front, but he didn't have any gel. He was buff, but the suits he wore fit just right.

"What did he do to you? Kelsey you were the happiest girl in the world when I was with you. Happy as can be, but now you have this hurt look in your eyes. What's wrong?" Emilio was always able to tell when I wasn't my best, and I was never able to lie to him about it.

He sat up in his seat and reached for my right hand that I had resting on the table. As soon as I felt his touch I pulled my hand back. "Milo I want to do right by my husband," I mumbled, taking the same hand that he touched and used it to push my bang out of my face.

Nodding his head, he promised me that he didn't mean any harm. "I know you may not want to talk about it right now, but if you ever need me I am here."

"Thanks, but I need to get going. Thank you for everything. I'll look over your case some more and I will let you know everything that I find."

I knew I had to get out of there or something was going to happen that I couldn't take back. Picking up my purse and phone, I headed out the door. Emilio threw some money down on the table and followed me to the parking lot. He did drive so I guess he did have to leave as well.

"Kelsey, I swear I didn't mean to cause any problems." He caught me by the passenger side door of his Bentley Bentayga. "Look it's no secret that I still love you. I want to give us another shot and from the shit I've heard about your husband, you should want to as well."

His words pulled at my heart because of the simple fact that my husband's infidelities weren't a
secret to anyone. Anyone who didn't live under a rock knew that my husband fucked every bitch from Atlanta to Los Angeles and from Detroit to New Orleans. That shit hurt because I was really trying my hardest to make us work.

Again, he'd left me with nothing else to say. I just looked at him as he looked at me. He stood in front of me, close enough that his cologne filled my nostrils. I felt him inching closer, but my eyes never left his. I was searching for what he was looking at. I felt like he was looking into my soul, but I was trying to see why.

Before I knew it Milo's lips were against mine and I was opening my mouth to let his tongue in. I felt so free and so refreshed. I felt like a freshman in high school getting kissed by a senior on the football team. "Stop," I finally came to my senses. Emilio slowly backed away from me.

"Look, let me take you back to your job. I am sorry that I forced myself on to you." He shook his head and waited for me to move out the way so he could open my door for me.

Shanking my head, I had to let him know that he wasn't the only at fault. "No, I didn't stop it at all. So we both committed a sin."

Emilio just shrugged as I got into the car I felt my phone vibrating in my clutch. I took it out and looked at the screen and noticed the number wasn't save, but it was a Los Angeles area code. "Hello?"

Only reason for an LA number to contact me would be with something concerning my husband. "Bitch, stay the fuck away from my man you hear me? King is mine bitch. You think you the shit because you are a fucking lawyer, but bitch you ain't. He has told me everything. I am his woman. Oh and the new drapes in the dining room are really cute."

Before I could get myself together to curse this random ass bitch out, the call disconnected and she was gone. My body started to shake because not only was this bitch fucking my man, but she had been to my house? The place where my child lives? The place I lay my head at night?

"Who was that," Emilio started the car and looked over at me. I had thrown the phone down on the floor and tried to shield my tears from him. The out-cry that came along with tears were enough to be heard outside of the car. "Kelsey, what's wrong?"

Emilio had stopped the car in the middle of the parking lot and got out and ran to my side. My cry had been so hard that my voice got stuck in my throat. "I'm so fucking tired Emilio. I am. I have done everything I could to make this marriage work. I have. I gave him a baby. I wasn't ready for a child, but he wanted it so he got it. I got back in church to get closer to God. I don't go out any more. I don't do anything besides work and take care of home."

As Milo wrapped his arms around me, I continued to let everything out. "That's the problem Kelsey. When put everything into everybody else, but you never take time for Kelsey. You have to have time for yourself baby." He kissed my forehead.

This shit wasn't supposed to happen to me. I had tried to live my life the right way, but I seem to face trouble everywhere I turn.

# Five

## King

Yesterday wore a nigga out. Having Kemarr at the studio was more than a nigga could handle so I had to call Lani over there to watch her while I laid down two tracks. Lani didn't seem to mind, but the bitch did get a fucking attitude when I told her we weren't fucking because I had my child with me.

I left the studio about a quarter to nine and Marri was knocked out. All I had to do was bathe her and lay her down. Hell her chunky ass ate all day, so I knew she wasn't hungry.

My wife decided that it would be cool for her to get home a little after ten last night. She thought a nigga was sleep, but I watched her ass text in her phone for an hour after she got out the shower. Ain't nobody up that late at night, but a nigga that was expecting some ass. Hell, I should know.

When I awoke this morning, her ass was in the shower so I had taken the time to see who the fuck she was texting all last night, but when I went to open her phone, it asked me for a passcode. Since I got with Kelsey her phone has never had a passcode, so what was so different now.

My breathing became heavier because I felt like my wife was betraying me. Just as I was about to put her phone back down where I got it from, a text came through.

*"I pray you are having a better day today. Call me if you need me,"* was all that E. Gustavo sent. My mind was going numb at the fact that my wife could really be out here giving what's mine to another nigga.

As soon as I heard the water from the shower stop, I placed her phone back down where I got it. I was going to get my chance to address her, but I was going to see how the shit played out first. If she was going to act cool, so was I, but if she had a stank ass attitude, so was I.

"Good morning," I greeted her with a smile as she went over to the bed and lotion her soft caramel skin. Kelsey didn't say shit to me as if she couldn't hear me. "Good morning, Kelsey." I repeated myself, louder, but she still didn't respond to me.

Anger took control of my body and soul because I flashed out on my wife. I stomped my feet over to her and yanked her arm so that she could turn around and face me. The smug look of her face said that I disgusted her and that pissed me off even more and I just wanted to beat that shit off her face.

"Get the fuck off of me you cheating bastard! I want you and your shit out of my fucking house!" She screamed and yanked her arm back from me. "I swear to God I'm through with you. I want a fucking divorce!"

Before I knew it I had pushed Kelsey to the floor and climbed on top of her pinning her down by her wrists. I stared at her face and I knew that she meant the words that she'd said and I could also see the hurt that she was feeling. No matter how she felt, she wasn't leaving me. I took my vows seriously when I said for better or for worse and until death itself did us apart. My breathing grew harder as I tightened my grip around her small wrists. I couldn't move, my emotions wouldn't allow me to.

"King, let me go," Kelsey said slightly above a whisper, trying her hardest to stop her voice from cracking.

"You not fucking leaving me!" I screamed loud enough for that shit to sink into her brain. Kelsey began to try to move to loosen the grip I had on her, but of course my damn near 350 lbs. out did her 175 lbs.

"Daddy stop," Kemarr came to the side of us and squatted down trying to remove my hands from her mother's arm.

I was so wrapped with anger I didn't even notice the door open for my child to come in. Hell I didn't know she was awake. Kemarr's voice made me realize what the fuck I was doing and I stood up and held out my hand to help Kelsey up, but she smacked my hand out of the way and got up herself.

Once Kelsey was up, Marri clung to her mother's leg. Looking at me with a sort of fear in her eyes. In that moment I knew that I had most likely lost my family and the only person I had to blame was myself.

"King, just get your stuff and get out of the house." She leaned down to pick up Marri. Instantly Marri started to wipe the tears from her mother's face. That shit made me feel even worse.

"I'm sorry Baby please. Please, just give me another chance. I am begging you please don't give up on me. I know I don't deserve it, but baby just give me another chance to do right by you." I walked over to her, reaching my arm out for her and she flinched. I made my wife flinch.

Kelsey just shook her head and walked past me, leaving me in the room alone.

# Six

## Kelsey

Three weeks, two days, four hours, and twenty-three minutes had passed since my husband had moved out of our home and into our first condo across town. He's called every day, multiple times a day, trying to apologize for his actions, but I still was hurt. How the fuck could he cheat on me, have the bitch in my home, and then have the nerve to put his hands on me.

Every night since then, Kemarr and I have been sleeping in my bed together because I didn't want to be alone. The judge in Emilio's case had decided to dismiss it because mysteriously the only witness that they had disappeared. I didn't want to question him about it, but I knew for a fact that he had a hand in whatever happened to her.

He and I had begun to get closer and it felt so good to have someone to spend time with and feel at ease. Although I hadn't introduced him to Kemarr yet, he always called me to make sure that I had everything I needed for myself and her. Even when I told him I was good, he still dropped off a wad of cash once a week.

"So what are you going to do now?" Harmonie asked as she and I browsed around the Burberry store in Lenox. Kemarr was taking school pictures in a couple of days so I wanted to have my baby looking fresh.

I had finally decided to tell Harmonie about the fight and the fact that he had moved out the house. She seemed to be happy about the situation, but then again she started disliking King a long time ago when she saw him coming out of the Hilton with some bitch. She wanted me to leave then, but she should have known I wouldn't have been so quick to move when I was seven months pregnant.

"I don't know. Milo has still been coming around more, but I don't even know how I feel about that either. With Kemarr and all, I don't want to do anything that'll mess with her head." I looked down at my phone seeing that I had about two hours before I had to picked my child up.

"Well Kels you know I loved Milo, but on some real shit, I want you to be happy. I feel like you aren't yourself anymore. I know people grow and change, but you don't get out anymore or anything." Harmonie and I were different. She was always the one who loved going out and shaking her ass in the club. I was always in VIP chair dancing because I hated the crowds. Thankfully with my family name ringing bells in the streets, we were able to get special treatment in the clubs starting at seventeen.

I did listen to what Harm was saying though. Since I got married I became totally submissive only keeping my job as something for me. "Well we'll have a girl's night or something." Harm agreed almost instantly, allowing us to leave the subject of my misery and on to spending money.

Harmonie was an accountant and owned her own firm. To say that she'd only been open for only two years her business was grossing a staggering million dollars a year due to the fact that she took on a hospital's account; so when she and I got together to shop believe money was being dropped.

After leaving Burberry with Kemarr's dress, we shopped around the mall to get an outfit for Kemarr's party. We left the mall and grabbed a bite to eat before heading our separate ways and I went

to go get Kemarr from school.

Stepping into Little Blessings, it looked like an actual school instead of a day care. As much as we paid of tuition it should look just as it did; clean and well organized. I headed to the gym where all the kids were held while they waited to be picked up.

I looked around the gym and I couldn't spot my toddler. "Mrs. Winter, where is Kemarr?" I questioned her teacher. I knew damn well they hadn't let my child wonder off.

"Mrs. Taylor, Kemarr's father came picked her up around ten this morning. I assumed you knew." She placed her hand over her heart as she informed me of the fact that my husband came got my child and I had no idea.

My pressure was rising and I felt that shit every step of the way. How could he come get my child and not tell me? I never kept him from Kemarr not once and now he just took her? What if I had something important planned?

"I'm going to beat the fuck out that nigga," I screamed to myself as I turned the key in the ignition. I pressed a few buttons on the screen of my car and it called out King's number.

*"Hey you've reached Yung Kane. I can't answer my phone right now, but if you need me immediately call my manager or my wife \*beep\*."* After hearing this shit for the fourth time I decided to leave a voicemail.

"Kane I don't know who the fuck you think you are playing with, but one thing about it and two mutha fucking things for sure when it comes down to Kemarr Marie Taylor, I plays no games. You better call me back and fast, letting me know where the fuck you are with my child," I screamed as I beat my hand on the steering wheel.

As the cars passed me, I knew they all thought I was crazy, but who cared about them. I drove to our old condo that King had been staying at off of Peachtree. The memories that this house had made me love it and hate it at the same time. It was where King and I spent our first night as a married couple. It was where we hung up his first gold album, but it was also the place where we first put our hands on each other. It was the first place I cried after I'd caught King cheating for the first time.

"Evening Mrs. Taylor," the staff greeted me as I walked into the lobby. I smiled and nodded my head. I had one goal in mind and that going to the house and seeing if my child was there. The elevator brought me up the eighteenth floor where only my apartment was. Each of the eighteen floors housed only one apartment and King just had to be on the top floor.

Once I entered the home using my key, I stormed in only to find it was empty. I walked all around just to make sure. The only shit I saw was King's dirty clothes on the bathroom floor. Checking my phone for a missed call and there was none, so I called again this time leaving even more of a vulgar message.

I knew my child was safe with her father, but it was the fact that I had no idea where she was that was killing me. Being as much of a helicopter mom as I was, I needed to know what Kemarr was doing every hour of the day.

Making my way home, after checking the studio, I took a hot shower and decided to ask Milo to come over to keep me company while I waited by the phone for King to call me back. He came over in a matter of minutes after I explained to him what was going on and he even came baring a bottle of red wine.

"How long have you been waiting?" Milo asked as we sat on the sofa drinking. I shrugged my shoulders and reached for my phone off of the coffee table and grabbed my phone, tabbing the home button to see the time. It was now six-thirty.

"Four hours. Four freaking hours." I kissed my teeth and readjusted myself on the sofa so that I was completely facing Milo and both of my feet were up with my knees in my chest.

Even with everything on my brain I still couldn't deny his beauty. The way his facial hair looked as if his barber used a protractor to cut it. It had a perfect angle from his sideburns to his jawline. His hair looked as if he had run his fingers through it and it actually stayed and the way I saw his muscles through his white button down, made my nipples hard.

"I can only imagine where your mind is." Emilio reached his hand over hand rubbed it against my foot. "You know I always think about what if we had kids." He placed his wine glass down on the side table and then gently pulled my leg from under me and into his lap so he could massage my feet.

The feelings that he was causing me to have were so wrong, but they felt so right. I was a married woman, a mother, a professional, a Christian. There was no way I should be feeling this way towards a man I left so long ago. "I think they would be just as pretty as Kemarr, but they would look more like me and have my jet black hair and nose. They would have your smile and your brain."

As he continued to describe the children in his head a slight moan escaped my lips and I knew I was in too deep. "Milo stop, please." I pulled my foot back and finally snapped out of my trance.

"My bad Kelsey, I just was trying to relax you." I nodded my head and blushed just a little, trying to make light of the situation. Milo grabbed his glass and brought it to his mouth, watching me do the same. "I'm sorry for kissing you the other day. I miss you and it's killing me to see you like this over this fucking *stupido cagna*." His Italian accent was very heavy on that last part as if he called King a bitch.

"Don't mention it, but I understand how you feel. Just respect the fact that I do respect my vows and the fact that you were the one who sent me away telling me you couldn't have a wife in your lifestyle." Emilio didn't have anything to say after that. He just nodded his head and apologized for that.

He and I started to watch *Criminal Minds* on Netflix since Milo promised me that he wouldn't leave until I had word on where Kemarr was. I continued to call and text King, but still I didn't get a response. I knew he had seen and heard everything I left on his phone, so for him not to answer was flat out disrespectful.

"Mommy," I snapped out of my feelings when I heard my child running towards the living room. I quickly got up and met her and her father just as they were coming my way. Emilio stood up from the sofa, but he didn't come by us, he just watched.

I picked up my child and held her close. I felt a weight lift off of my shoulders knowing I had my child. "Man Kelsey I know you don't have no nigga in my fucking house," King snapped.

"Watch your language and he's a friend. You have had women all in my house. Not to mention you took my child from school and didn't bother to call me to let me know." I rolled my eyes as I placed Kemarr down on the ground.

"Mommy, Daddy took me to six flags." She pointed at her t-shirt. I noticed she had on a t-shirt, a pair of capris, and some Jordan's.

"That's nice baby. Go upstairs and wait for my mommy to come give you a bath." I smiled at her. "Kiss Daddy goodnight."

After they said their goodbyes and my child was upstairs I started. "You really got my fucked up, where is her uniform? Why would you randomly take her out of school to go to an amusement park?"

"Nah the real question is who the fuck is this white nigga standing in my house? Nigga who is you and what were you doing with my wife?" King stepped around me and headed over to Emilio.

From the outside you would easily think that King had this shit in the bag with his height, but Milo wasn't no punk nigga, he held his own. "Look here my man, you might want to watch who you are talking to."

They stared each other up and down for a few seconds daring the other to make a sudden move. When I saw both of their hands reaching towards their backs I had to jump in. Wasn't nobody dying in my shit. "Don't pull out a gun in the house where my child is. Bullets have no name. Emilio thanks for coming. I'll call you later," I turned to him and thanked him.

He let out a slight laugh and nodded his head. "Yea, Kelsey call me when you get rid of this *pagliaccio*." He came up for a hug and then walked out the door.

"Kelsey, what is wrong with you for having a man in my fucking house. You cheating on me?" King questioned standing in his spot as if he was going to do something.

I looked at him just as if he was really the clown that Milo had called him because right now he was making me laugh. As many bitches as he has fucked while we were married, he had the nerve to try and tell me anything about my life. "Nigga when you got bitches blowing my phone telling me how they like my new curtains, you shouldn't have shit to say. How did you get in my house anyway? I changed the locks and the code."

"The fuck you talking about? I ain't never had no bitch in the house we shared. I put that shit on my mama, and 0852 is always the code you go to if you can't think of anything else." King smacked and looked around the room thinking of something to say. "Kelsey look baby I am sorry. Let a nigga right his wrongs please. For Kemarr if you don't do it for me. Give her a chance to see her parents together."

"Don't use my child against me King." I flicked my wrist as I walked past him. "Get the fuck out of my house." I headed up the steps. I heard him follow me into the foyer. I paused at the top of the stairs to make sure his ass was leaving my house. He looked up and me and blew me a kiss before he walked out of the door. "And lock my door!" I screamed behind him.

# Seven

## Kelsey

"Well you know how I feel about divorce. You just don't do it. I mean your father and I have been through a hell of a lot, but I raised you right. A woman isn't meant to get married three and four times." My mother lectured through Facetime. I sat back in my office chair and watched her on my Mac computer screen.

My mother had called saying that she sensed that I was going through something and that she needed to talk to me. I ended up telling her everything that was going on with me, besides that fact that I was talking to Emilio again. Neither of our families liked the fact that we had mixed with the opposite race. They never physically stopped us, but they both were in our ears with different remarks that we didn't care to hear.

"Kelsey I love you so I just want the best for you. You and your brother are my world. I would tell him not to leave his wife too," she continued her speech. I shrugged my shoulders and sat up grabbing my phone when my phone lit up letting me know I had a text.

"Yea Ma, but this nigga cheated on me and had another woman in my house. That's so disrespectful." I never looked at her, but I read and replied to Emilio's text saying that he was just checking on me.

Once I sat my phone down I looked back at my mother. I swore we looked nothing alike. She had a deep chocolate complexion with nice full features and a heavier shape, but she only stood about five-foot-two. She was beautiful to say the least. People always said that she reminded them of a shorter Kelly Price.

"Kelsey Mikel, do you know how many times your father cheated on me? No it's not right, and to my knowledge he hasn't in about ten years, but still. Think about it baby girl, I never have to touch him again if I wanted to; everything is paid for and I have nothing to worry about; and if I did want to touch him he is my husband so I am not sinning." My mother was so set in her ways and I knew that there was no changing it, but I don't know if I was as strong as her. I can't just sit here. "And don't you go out there fighting bitches unless they touch you."

I couldn't talk to her anymore so I just told her I had an appointment and promised to call her later. She legit was blowing me and I was already aggravated after going pretty much all of yesterday not knowing the whereabouts of my child.

The end of the day had finally come, when I noticed the clock said three forty-five. Normal working hours were nine to five, but I worked eight-thirty to two-thirty in the office and whatever else I had to do would get done at home.

There was no rush for me to get home because King has asked if he could get Kemarr from school and of course I said it was ok. I would never keep my child away from her father, but I just wanted to know that he had her and that I would be able to get to her if something went wrong.

When I got to my truck in the garage there were a bouquet of yellow roses sitting on my
window shield. As scary as I was, I looked around my car to make sure there wasn't a bomb or some shit that I could see. When I did a full walk-around to make sure my tires weren't slashed.

"You are the only person I know that would see roses and think something bad," Emilio's voice came closer and closer to me. I jumped at the sound because I hadn't expected to see him since he told me he was busy.

"Emilio don't scare me like that," I placed my hand over my chest and rolled my eyes. He laughed at me and took the flowers off of my car. I hurried to open my door so I could place my briefcase in the car so I could grab my flowers. "These are so beautiful; I am guessing you got them for me?"

Hell I couldn't be too sure since I didn't see a card or anything. "Yes Kelsey. I figured after yesterday you could use something to brighten your day." He smiled like a big ass kid that'd just won the spelling bee.

I gave him a hug and thanked him for the nice gesture. "Have you eaten today?" I asked hoping he'd say no. I had a taste for a salad as I always did.

"Actually I did eat breakfast," he burst my bubble just that fast. "But I skipped lunch due to a meeting, so I am kind of hungry."

"Good, well come with me to Villa Rosa with me. They have great food and it is also happy hour."

"No need to say anymore," he laughed, accepting my invitation.

Since Emilio had used a driver to get to my office, he sent the driver home and rode with me. It felt just like old times, and that was something that I needed.

\*\*\*

### King

"Daddy, you gon come home and be happy with Mommy," Marri asked while she sat across from me eating her frozen yogurt. I placed my phone down on the table and looked at my child. She was way too smart to say she was only four years old, so I needed to watch how I said this.

"Kemarr, Mommy and I are going through grown folks stuff so I don't know when I'll be home, but it doesn't matter because I love you so much. I will do anything for you." I smiled, more so for myself because I felt like I had handled the situation well.

"You love me enough to come home?" See this was the shit I was talking about with Marri, her ass always had a million questions that I would usually leave up to her mother to answer.

"Eat your ice cream, Daddy gotta do something." There was no way I was going to answer that question. I wanted to go home and be with my wife, God himself knew I did, but Kelsey wasn't budging.

Kelsey had a nigga in our home yesterday and that shit was tugging at me because I had never
done that shit. No matter the dirt I did, I ain't never brought another bitch where my wife laid her head. "Kemarr, you know that man that was at the house last night? That white man."

"I don't know, but Mommy got a friend named Mr. Emily or something like that. I ain't never seen him, but Mommy told T' Harmonie that he gave her five-thousand dollars." She was like a little woman sitting there, spilling all this tea.

That shit made me hot as fuck. This bitch not only was cheating on me with a white nigga, but was fucking getting money from him too. Kelsey made bank as a lawyer, hell she even got a couple of rappers I know out of some hard time from drug charges. Not only did she have that money, but I paid for every fucking bill she had. This woman didn't even have to pay her own iTunes bill so there was no reason for her to be accepting money from another nigga.

After hearing that, I didn't want any more ice cream or nothing, I was ready to go. "Aye Marri, we'll get more ice cream later, I'm ready to go." I stood up from the table and waited for her to get up. "Nah fix that damn attitude. I don't like all that poutin'. You don't pay no bills so you don't have anything to be upset about."

"But why do we have to go? I was almost done. Can I eat it in the car?" Kemarr was slowly pushing in her chair and she had a little puppy dog look on her face. It was so hard to look at her pretty face and tell her no.

"Fine Kemarr, shit. Don't waste that in my car." I smacked mu lips and watched as she happy danced as she grabbed her ice cream from the table.

"I know, I know. You drive a very expensive car and it costs more than most people's homes. I ain't gon mess up your seats." She flicked her wrists and walked past me sticking a spoonful of rainbow sherbet in her mouth.

Since I had finished up my album earlier than expected, there was no reason for me to go to the studio so I headed to the condo. The condo was nice as hell. Two bedrooms, two and a half bathrooms, a balcony, a chef's kitchen, and view of the entire city. As nice as the shit was I had one memory that I couldn't get out of my head and I hated myself for it. Every night before I went to sleep I replayed me and Kelsey's first fight in my head. I would never forget myself for slapping her and I would never forget that she stabbed me in the chest.

Once inside of the house, Kemarr ran right to the living room and for the TV. All she did was watch videos of Selena Gomez, Taylor Swift, Fifth Harmony, and any other young pop star just to stand in the middle of the floor and have a concert.

I knew she could entertain herself so I headed to my room and decided to relax, smoke, and jot down some ideas for my mixtape. Although I was about to drop an album I needed something else that would keep my fans entertained while I prepared for my next album.

Being in the industry had taught me to always stay on my toes. Although I've only been in the game eight years, I have seen people at number one and the very next week they are forgotten about. I wanted to make sure that was never me. I was always dropping something whether it was free or had to be purchased, my fans always had something to vibe to.

Just as the weed started to sink into my system my phone started ringing. "Hello," I picked up, not even bothering to see who was calling me. Worst shit I could have done.

"Why haven't you been answering my calls, Kane? I need to talk to you it is an emergency." Leilani whined into the phone. Since Kelsey had kicked me out, I cut shit off with Lani so I could work on getting my shit together.

I rolled my eyes because I knew she was about to blow my fucking high. "Mane, what you want?" I leaned over to grab a bottle of water from my nightstand since my throat was dry.

"Fuck Kane why you acting like this? Whatever, I have to talk to you." She continued. In order to save whatever little of my high that I had left, I decided to allow her to come over to the condo. Although Kelsey used to lay her head here, she doesn't now so I ain't see a problem.

Lyrics were coming to me left and right and I was ready to lay down some tracks, but I knew I wanted to continue to master my shit so that I could drop some hot shit. I knew I wanted to have some features, it was just trying to figure out with who.

Not before long I got a text from Leilani telling me she was at the door. I slowly made my way out of my room and to the door. Kemarr was still having her own concert not even bothering to stop when she saw me enter the room. Her nosey ass did pause the TV when I opened the door and Leilani came into the apartment.

"Hey Babe," Lani tried to greet me with a kiss, but I curved the fuck outa her. That hoe knew better than to try some shit in front of my child. "Hey Marri," she waved at Kemarr with a smile.

"Daddy, Mommy know she over here at our condo?" Kemarr eyed Lani with a slight attitude. I did a slight laugh at how ruthless she was.

"Nah and she ain't gonna find out is she?" I closed the door behind Lani and stood there and waited for my child's response. She shook her head and turned back on her music, going back to doing what she was doing before Leilani interrupted our flow.

Lani followed me to my room and sat on the bed as if she had made herself at home. I laid back down in my spot and waited for her to start talking. "I went to the doctor a week ago and they told me I was pregnant."

I picked up my phone and started strolling through Twitter. "So who all you been fucking?" It was no secret that Leilani got around so as far as I was concerned her child could be for about six other niggas, if she was even pregnant.

"Really Kane, you know this is your baby as well as I do. I came over here to tell you it was time to leave your wife." She stood up from the bed and threw her purse down. "We have to be a family; I have a reputation to keep up."

I started laughing because I was trying to understand where she thought her rep was so good that people would be surprised if she had a baby with no baby daddy. "Lani you knew damn well I ain't never tell you I would leave my wife for you."

"Kane don't do me that. You know you love me, so don't try it." She started with the water works. "Please Baby, can we work something out. I still owe my record label two more albums and I can't do that by myself."

"Women do it every day." I knew I was being hard on her, but I really didn't see where this was my problem. "Look, I'll give you the money to get rid of it, but you can't keep that shit. I want no parts of it. I already have a child with my wife and she's more than enough. And don't try to get slick thinking you are going to keep it and I'm going to feel guilty and want to help you because I'm not." I stood up from my bed and reached for my wallet and handed her whatever cash I had in there.

She sat back down on my bed and started to cry even harder. "I don't need your fucking money Kane, I need you. We need you. I didn't make this child by myself so you can't expect me to raise it by myself."

"And I don't that is why I'm giving you the fucking money Leilani. Take it and do what the fuck you have to do to get rid of the fetus." My voice slightly rose because she was starting to annoy me.

Maybe I was wrong for telling her to kill a baby, but I couldn't allow a baby to come into the picture when I was trying to work on my relationship. I knew Kelsey would cut my dick off herself and then stab me in the chest for the second time.

When Leilani seemed to not stop her crying antics I sat down on the bed and turned on the TV. I wasn't going to try and be nice like I gave a fuck because I didn't. I made it clear from the jump when I met her, I was a married man and all I was looking for was to get my dick wet. Hell and this bitch told me that she just enjoyed having dick inside of her.

After a couple of minutes of watching **Catfish,** Leilani finally stood to her feet and got herself together. Standing to her feet and throwing her purse of her shoulder she spoke, "Tell your wife of I will."

"Bitch the last person you want to threaten is me."

# Eight

## Kelsey

The day was finally here. My baby was now five years old and I knew that her date of birth had to be celebrated just like any pop star's day should be. I had rented out a production studio and hired everything that we needed to make a video. I had planned everything out and Kemarr and her friends were going to go in groups of five, pick their favorite song, and make a lip-synch video to the music.

There was hair and make-up, wardrobe, and a red carpet entrance with a photo backdrop. I got a photo booth station set up for the kids who were waiting on their turn in front of the camera. Hell I had even hired a dance choreographer to help with some moves.

Needless to say, this party cost me an arm and a leg and because I didn't pay bills or anything, everything I made was for me; so I was able to go all out on this party. Emilio offered to help, so he got the party catered by Popeye's because its Kemarr's favorite. He ordered a five tier cake, a tier for each year she'd been alive. He even had Kemarr set to arrive in a limo. I couldn't thank him enough. You would think King would've offered to pay for something the way he had been posting my child all over his social media accounts like she had her own account to see them.

"Marri where are y'all?" I asked her through Harmonie's phone since she rode with the kids while I was on site getting everything together. Mothers were starting to arrive and I needed to have everything perfect.

"We picking up Jayden, we are coming. Bye." She hung up in my face, leaving me looking at the phone like I was trippin'.

The limo was set to pick up each of the fourteen other kids as their parents and myself waited for them to arrive. I mingled with the other mothers as we discussed our children and they all told me how over the top this party was, but they all loved it. I was beginning to get anxious, but the feeling of disgust come over me when I spotted King and his best friend, Johnny, walked into the building. Johnny was cool people, but he was a hoe so I wasn't too fond of him and my husband hanging together.

I walked over to meet them because although King, Johnny, and I knew that the deal was, no one else knew and that was the way I wanted to keep it. People didn't need to know I had problems going on in my house. It wasn't that I was trying to act like I didn't have any problems or as if I was better than the next person, I just didn't like a lot of opinions in my business.

"Where are the kids?" King asked as he brought me in for a hug. I acted in my role and hugged him back. His scent did something to me, but my head didn't let me forget his mistakes.

"They are on their way here. Hey Johnny." I greeted him with a wave. Like I said, I wasn't too fond of him.

King nodded his head and Johnny spoke back before we walked over and mingled with the parents. Not too many fathers showed up, which was normal for a kid's birthday party. The father's that did show up were somewhat affiliated with King in the music industry.

I motioned for the waiter to come around with the mimosas for the parents. I was tired of not having a drink in my hand.

"Hello," I answered my phone grabbing a mimosa from the tray.

"Hey darling. I was calling to see how the party was going." Emilio spoke on the other line. His words warmed my heart because it showed that her cared. I looked around the room to see the adults seemed to be enjoying themselves so I already knew the children would as well.

"Everything is beautiful. Thank you for everything," I blushed into the phone. I asked about his day and when was I going to see him. Although I wasn't trying to get emotionally involved with Emilio as of yet, he really and truly just made me feel good.

As I was caking on the phone, I felt a hand rest upon my shoulder. "The kids are here." King whispered in my ear.

"Aye, let me call you back." I told Milo before I hung up and stuck my phone in the back pocket of my black short romper.

I turned my attention to the kids who were walking in, stopping to take pictures on the red carpet. Kemarr was really feeling herself. This morning when she woke up, I decided to let her naturally curly hair go free and I added a small piece of a pink clip-in.

"So you were talking to that nigga while I was in the same room? I know I've done a lot, but I at least tried to keep some sort of line that I wouldn't cross." King was right on my ass as I made my way over to the kids.

"Then how the bitch know about my curtains?" I took a sip of my glass and waited for him to answer my question. This nigga was really trippin' if he thought he was justified by anything he did. A cheater was a cheater, was a cheater.

King was about to say some slick shit out his mouth, but Kemarr ran over to us. "Mommy, look at all of this stuff. It's so pretty. Thank you," she jumped up and down as she thanked me with her hands wrapped around my waist.

"No problem Marri, anything for Momma's baby." I rubbed her back and bent down to give her a kiss.

King was standing there waiting for her to thank him, but she almost didn't until he cleared his throat. "Thank you Daddy. I'm a pop star and I'm making a video." She reached for him to pick her up.

She gave him a kiss on his cheek and that did him all the good. I kept my smile on as he acted as if he put together and paid for this entire party. I was going to let Kemarr continue to think her father was made of gold until she saw for herself.

The lady that I had hired to make sure that everything ran smoothly today came and told everyone that it was time for the kids to start getting ready for their shoots. Kemarr hopped down from her father's arms and ran over to her friends.

I spotted my best friend over by the food table and decided I would go make me a plate too. "Aye, Kelsey can I ask you something?" King stopped me in my tracks.

"What, King?"

"Would you come to my album release party?" He stood there with his hands behind his back like a child. I eyed him up and down and remembered that if I wanted my marriage to work, then I was going to have to get over my anger and try it once again.

"Yea, I'll be there," I smiled, seductively. No matter what, I could never lie and say my husband wasn't the finest nigga I have ever seen. He just did something to me; nigga made my clit jump in my panties.

The rest of the party was spent making sure Kemarr had the best time she possibly could. She made sure everyone knew it was about her, and her only. She appeared in all three of the videos, making sure she was the lead, and she also tried to be in almost every picture someone took.

King surprised us all when he presented her with her very own custom Barbie Jeep and Barbie four-wheeler. Kemarr went wild, telling everyone on King's Instagram that *he was the best daddy in the entire world*. Of course that led to my husband adding a caption saying something to the effect of no one ever being able to take his place in his child's life.

### Emilio

"Boss, we need you now," Antonio rushed into my office. I never looked up at my computer, I just nodded my head. "We have Harrison's ass down there."

Now if he would have said those words in the beginning, I would have been ready to get my ass up and go see what the fuck he was talking about. I exited out what was on my computer and got up from my chair.

Antonio led me through the casino and down to the basement. I had just gotten back to Atlantic City and I was determined to catch up with every nigga that owed me a dollar. I was a beast behind my money and I was known for making examples out of niggas so niggas usually had my shit when I asked for it, but Harrison had been late not once, but twice and that shit was unacceptable.

"So this the pussy that owes me $150k? Friend, you were really good at hiding, but I'm a beast when it comes down to hunting my prey. Most people would have never thought to look for you at your ex-wife's cousin's house, but once I saw that your weekly calls had suddenly come to a stop, I knew that it had to be looked into."

I started as soon as I walked into the room and I was pleased with the sight of him not being harmed. I wanted him to anticipate the thought of torture coming to him because that was the worst pain.

"I promise you I was going to pay you the money, but when I got it. I had some problems and shit got backed up, but when I got it, you were the first person I was coming to see." Harrison pleaded in his thick Russian accent, but it fell upon deaf ears.

"Y'all hear this guy talking about what he **was** going to do? Can someone please explain to him that my bills don't get paid with the money he **was** going to pay me?" I laughed, a little harder than I should have. People always killed me when they spoke about things they were going to do, knowing damn well they never had any intentions to do it.

Harrison tried to join in on the laugh too like he didn't understand the severity of the situation. At the end of the day, my money was missing and that was a fucking problem. "Just give me twenty-four hours to come up with the money."

I thought about being nice enough to allow him to do that, but the quartier in me wouldn't allow me to actually be that kind. "My dear friend, I will give you that chance. You all turn the lights off on this pussy for twenty-four hours."

That nigga was going to have twenty-four hours to come up with my money with his dreams because he damn sure in the hell wasn't about to get a chance to go in the streets and run off again. Harrison was going to die and now he had twenty-four hours to think about it.

Telling Kelsey I wasn't in the streets anymore wasn't entirely true. Although I don't run the streets anymore, I still had my hand in the pot. Basically, I allowed people to do my dirty work and I just collected my money. Although I made myself a legal millionaire with the casino, I was damn near worth two-hundred million dollars if you included my drug empire.

As I passed through the casino, I decided to check out the club. We were having Leilani preform tonight and I knew she was going to keep the crowd on their feet and spending money at the bar.

Her music was a mixture between Lil Kim and Fantasia. She was nasty as hell, but yet it was filled with so much soul. It also didn't hurt that she was built like a Coke bottle. She had one of those asses that just jiggled when she walked and clapped when she bounced it.

"Mr. Gustavo would you like something to drink," one of my cocktail waitresses asked me as soon as I stepped into the club. I shook my head and continued to walk to the side of the stage. Leilani was on stage with the tightest black cat-suit and a pair thigh-high blue stiletto boots. The bitch was fine.

The crowd sung along with her to every song she performed. She even allowed a couple of fans to come on stage and preform with her. When they were done, she walked down with them and jammed with the crowd. She put on a good show and that made me ok with the damn two-hundred and fifty thousand she was asked for.

"So you are going to come watch my show and not tell me how you liked it Papi?" Leilani came up behind me as I stood at the bar. Her set was done and now the club was back to dancing to the latest music.

Slightly turning towards her I looked at her, "You did ok." I knew Leilani had to be one of those women who thought she was hot shit and I was not going to continue to fuel the flame. She had a nice body and a pretty face, but I was old enough to know that a body and a face would get old.

"Papi, you know I was better than *ok*. I was hot shit." She rubbed my arm through my suit jacket and damn near licked my ear with the tip of her tongue. This bitch was nasty, and I was low-key feeling it.

"You know Ms. Leilani you seem pretty full of yourself." I had fully tuned to face her to get a better look at her. She wasn't that tall because even with her heels on, I was looking down at her. I knew she had to be no taller than five-one barefoot.

I hadn't had sex in so long, holding off for Kelsey who seemed not to be interested, so my shit was throbbing at the sight of her curves. "You seem to be full of yourself, and I'm trying to be full of you too."

That was all I needed to hear. I bit my lip and whispered in her ear to meet me in the penthouse suite in fifteen minutes. Leilani agreed and went off to her dressing room. I headed upstairs in order to make sure that it was as clean as it should have been.

As soon as I got into the room, I was pleased with everything I saw so I headed to the master of the two rooms and dimed the lights with the tablet that was installed into the wall. I opened the curtains so that the view of the city could be the backdrop of the night.

Right on the dot, fifteen minutes later there was a soft knock on the door. I slowly walked over to the door and opened it for her. The bitch was standing there with a silk robe on and once I opened the door, she let it fall to the floor, reveling she wasn't wearing anything underneath besides the furry slipper heals that were on her feet.

"You like what you see, Papi?" Leilani brushed past me and entered the suite. I watched as her ass jiggled as she walked. I closed the door and followed behind her to the room that I had **set up** for us.

I walked up behind her and rubbed my hands against her warm sun-kissed skin. I moved her two braids out the way as I started to kiss on her neck and reach my hand down to play with her pussy. I was pleased when I found her to be wet. "Emilio, make love to me."

She almost caused me to stop when she called my name since I had never given it to her, but when she bent over in front of me and revealed her gold, all thoughts went out the window.

# Nine

## Kelsey

"Why are we here again," Harmonie asked as we sat in the VIP section of club Tequila for King's album release party.

"Because my husband asked me to be here," I replied, rolling my eyes. I knew she was just being protective of me, but fuck I wouldn't have asked her ass to come if I would have known that she would have been so damn aggravating. Since I picked her up she had been asking me if I was sure that I wanted to make my marriage work.

Harmonie didn't bother to reply to me, instead she grabbed a hold of the waitress and asked for a bottle of Henny to be delivered to our section. I looked around the very packed club and was so proud of King's success.

Everyone who was anyone in the industry or the state of Georgia was in the building celebrating my husband. He was busy entertaining the crowd as he did best while I sat in our section and looked cute. The people who were all in our section were out on the floor while Harm and I sipped and looked.

"Baby, come here. Dance with me." King came into the section and grabbed me by my hand. I looked down at the iridescent spandex-like leather with matching bralette and Cruel Crystal Giuseppe's that I had worn, and I knew I defiantly wasn't dressed for dancing, but I obliged his request and followed him on to the dance floor.

Just as we were walking to the floor, Nicky Da B's "Gots" roared through the club and as soon as I heard it, I bent over in front of my husband and made my ass move. The little New Orleans that I did have in me, lived for bounce music.

King grabbed a hold of my waist as I made the outfit I had on work for me. A small crowd started to form and of course they only encouraged me to go harder, and I did, making my ass go faster and faster in a circle. Then suddenly another girl came into the circle and started to dance, making this shit a competition.

"Awe shit, Leilani has entered the ring. Who you rolling with? The King's wife or America's firmest piece of ass? I got something else for y'all," DJ Slim Rick screamed over the mic. He switched it from one bounce song to another.

All I head to hear was, "touch your body, feel it in your soul" by Wildboy Woody and my body started moving. I walked and shook my ass. The crowd was going crazy. Leilani had her hands on her knees, but she was twerking. You cannot twerk to bounce music; you have to shake or pounce.

So as my ass pushed her out the way, I squatted down and continued to shake. Once I was finished, I walked over to my husband who was smiling from ear to ear. "I haven't seen you cut up like that since we were dating," he grabbed me by my waist and kissed my lips.

"Alright, alright! Kelsey Taylor has just proven to everybody in this bitch, that's how you keep your man! Ladies, let me see y'all work!" The DJ started again then he put on *"Work"* by Rhianna and the ladies started twerking to the beat.

King and I made our way back over to our section where Harmonie was sitting, talking to some nigga who I'd never seen before, but he was fine as hell. As soon as we sat down, King started feeling all over my thighs and kissed all on my neck. It honestly felt good to feel affection from my husband again.

It didn't even matter that we were in a club, and it was packed. Hell it didn't even matter that my best friend and some nigga were less than fifteen feet away from us. In that moment we were alone in alone in the world. As he rubbed my thigh and nibbled on my ear and I giggled like I was in middle school, our relationship was slowly healing.

"Hey y'all." When we heard the voice, King and I slowly stopped and turned our heads. "Kane, you not gonna introduce me to your wife? Especially after she just beat me at twerking." Leilani laughed as she reached her hand out for me to shake.

"Baby, this is Leilani. Leilani, this is my beautiful wife, Kelsey." King introduced us, but he clung to me as if he wanted her to know how much affection he felt towards me.

Leilani took a seat right next to me and started talking to me like we had known each other for years, and I was digging her vibe. Just as we were about to exchange phone numbers so we could meet for lunch or something, King got up and said we had to leave.

"Wait, hold on King," I was trying to get my phone out of my clutch.

"Kelsey, come on now. My sister's been called into the hospital. She can't watch Kemarr anymore." King stood up from the white sofa we were sitting on and becked for me to hurry up.

Once he mentioned our child, I was ready. "Girl, I'll catch you next time." I smiled at her and got up from the sofa as well. I motioned to Harmonie that it was time to go and she mouthed that she was leaving with the nigga sitting next to her.

In the car we were silent. King drove as if he had built up aggression or some shit. When we got to his sister's home, he threw the Panamera into park and hopped out to go get Kemarr. He was staring to get on my nerves because of the simple fact that we went from having such a good time to just being cold.

To say it was two in the morning, I expected my child to be carried out of her aunt's home sleeping in her father's arms. Instead, she walked out holding her father's hand and talking.

"Mommy you had fun at the party," was what she said when she first got into the car.

I watched my husband close the door behind her as Kemarr put on her seat belt. It was really bothering me that he didn't keep her booster seat in his car like I did. Talking about some, *"It be jockin' my style."*

"Yes Kemarr Mommy did, but why aren't you sleepy?" I turned around in my seat and looked at her. Her hair was loose all over her head and she was wearing a big white t-shirt and flip-flops. I made a mental note to call my sister-in-law in the morning and ask her where the hell my child's clothes were.

"Mommy, it isn't a school night. It's Friday so I don't have school tomorrow. T't Chantae said that I could stay up and watch TV with her." I nodded my head and turned to my husband. He knew what I was about to say so he answered my unasked question.

"I'll talk to her about it tomorrow. I did tell Chantae that Marri needed to be asleep by nine. Maybe she forgot." He never looked over at me, but he raised his hand as if that was supposed to stop me from speaking.

"Yea, and ask her about my child clothes and why I sent her with her hair combed, but I get her back with her hair all over her head." I rolled my eyes. Chantae and I were really cool at first, but she was the type that her big brother couldn't do any wrong in her eyes. So when she decided to walk her ass up in my firm and demand that I started being submissive to her brother, I was done.

All night I had been telling myself that I would let King stay at the house tonight, but with the little attitude he had been giving throughout the car ride, I started to second guess myself. The sensitive little girl within me decided to let him stay because it was better for him to be in my bed than in the bed of another bitch.

King quickly got his act together when he found out that he was allowed to stay at the house, tonight. He was on his best behavior when we got Kemarr into bed and didn't even try to fight when we got by ourselves in the room.

After we both showered, we got in the bed and laid there. I was on my side and he was on his. I didn't know if I wanted him to touch me or not, but the fact that he didn't automatically reach for me, pulled at my heart. Getting to our happy place was going to be harder than I expected, but I was willing to put in the work. I prayed to God my marriage didn't fail, but if we weren't meant to be I prayed he gave me a sign that I could clearly see.

# Ten

## King

Leilani had been blowing up my phone all two days since the night of the party and I have yet to answer because I truly didn't know how I would react once I spoke or saw her. The bitch had made my blood boil when she came over and started talking to my fucking wife.

For the past two nights Kelsey had been allowing me back in the house so I've been walking on eggshells. It killed me at night not to reach over to her side and wrap her in my arms, but I knew she probably didn't want to be bothered, and to be honest I couldn't blame her. I'd hurt her past the point of redemption so for her to even let me in the bed was enough for me.

After we brought Marri to school, we had a meeting with our pastor for counselling. We were quiet the entire car ride besides tell Marri to have a great day and ordering Kelsey's daily Starbucks.

Once I parked in front of the church, I turned the car off before getting out and jogging over to Kelsey's side to open her door. She stepped out looking like a bag of money. I smiled to myself knowing that she was mine and nobody else could have her. Besides that little texting incident, Kelsey had never given me a reason to think that she would cheat on me, so I wasn't really worried about it.

"Morning Brother and Sister Taylor. Pastor Tucker is in his office waiting on you all," the pastor's secretary greeted us when we walked into the office area of the church. I nodded my head at her and continued to walk.

New Hope and Spirit Baptist Church was the perfect match for my family. I wanted to go to a large church and Kelsey wanted to attend a church that wasn't so big, and this church was perfectly in the middle.

Pastor's office was set up real official like with the sitting area right by the window overlooking the church's garden. "Morning Pastor," Kelsey and I greeted the man of God in unison.

"Well it isn't the lovely couple. You know I still remember when you all joined the church and when we christened Kemarr." Pastor was a very talkative man and he was always reminding us of what he remembered.

We laughed and took a seat in the sitting area and I prepared for whatever was to come because I knew it may get real heavy. I looked over at my wife who sat unbothered drinking her damn coffee.

"So what brings you all to see me today?" Pastor Tucker asked, taking a seat in front of us.

"We are having problems in our marriage and we need help." I answered the question as honestly as I could.

Pastor Tucker nodded his head and looked over to Kelsey who had sat her drink down, but was fixing her Celine bag on side of her. "Mrs. Taylor, you seem as if you are trying to avoid talking or something to that extent."

Kelsey faced him and rubbed her palms against her thighs. "I don't know if I would call it that, but like King said, we are having trouble. We need help, but I don't know if I want it."

"Can you elaborate on this please," Pastor sat up in his chair. I looked at my wife and I knew what was about to come. I couldn't blame her for the way she felt, but I just wished that she didn't just jump into it so quickly.

She took a deep breath before she went on any further. "I know divorce is a sin and I also know that I am supposed to be with my husband for better or for worse, but how long am I supposed to stay with a man who continues to defile our martial bed?"

"Pastor I have never slept with another woman in our bed or our home," I cut her off trying to defend myself.

"What I was saying was you defiled what our marriage represents. Every time you stick yourself into a woman that is not me, you are defiling our marital bed and I am sick of it. Pastor I am tired of doing what I am supposed to do as a wife. Up until recently I had never denied him of sex because I do believe that a woman should fully submit, but I'm not a damn idiot."

The tears were rolling down her cheeks and it gave me sour feeling in my stomach. I caused all of that hurt, for no reason, but I couldn't stop myself. I've tried, but I couldn't resist it when a fine ass woman walked past and she was fine as hell.

As Kelsey continued her venting, I was feeling smaller and smaller because she made me realize all the things she'd sacrificed for me and all the times she came through for me knowing I wasn't going to return the favor. "So do you want to fix your marriage?" Pastor asked Kelsey the question while I passed her a box of Kleenex.

We waited in silence while Kelsey wiped her face thinking of an answer, but she crushed me when she said, "I truly don't know."

"Baby, Kelsey I am so sorry that I wasn't man enough to face up to be the man of God that you and Kemarr needed me to be. I love you with everything inside of me. Please just five me one more chance to prove to you that I can get it right. I know you can't fully forgive me right now, but just think about it.

I placed my arms around her and she slowly moved out of my embrace. "I think what we need to do here is start over. It sounds like neither one of you is remembering to keep God as the head of your lives. He has to be the head so that everything else can fall in line BEHIND him."

My ears were listening to him, but my brain and my eyes were focused on how Kelsey was still crying and as much as she tried to stop, she couldn't.

# Eleven

## Kelsey

"Sharmane I need you to bring me the file for the new client that Mr. Michaelson sent me," I called out to her though the intercom. After she told me she would, I went back over the files on my desk.

Not only had I forgotten to ask my husband if he was going to perform at the company's event, I'd also forgotten to send the list of invitees to the party planner so I had to quickly email them to her.

"Here you are Kels," Sharmane sat the file down on my desk. I thanked her and started to look over it. "It isn't a big case. It is a simple marijuana case, but the client's status is why you have the case."

"Is this Leilani the singer?" I looked at the name and decided to ask since I was given this case because of the person's status. Leilani Rivera had quite the misdemeanor RAP Sheet. It seemed as if she had a number of domestic violence incidences, but this was her first run in with marijuana.

"Yes ma'am it is, but look I'm about to head out for lunch. Are you coming or do you want me to bring you something back?" Sharmane asked halfway out of the door.

"Grilled chicken salad with salt and pepper please." I yelled behind her because she legit was out of the door by now.

As I continued to look at the case I figured it would pretty much be a piece of cake. Basically I was about to make free money because the judge presiding over her court date owed me a couple of favors.

I decided to give Leilani a call and let her know I was over her case and my plan as to how I was going to get her off. I figured that she'd be happy to know that her case could be swept under the rug.

"Hello," she answered in a very thick Hispanic accent. I thought it was cute because she looked **Black** on the outside, but she really wasn't.

"Hello this is Kelsey Taylor of J.D Michaelson's Law Firm, am I speaking to Ms. Leilani Rivera?"

"Hey Kelsey! Yea this Leilani, remember we met at Kane's release party." Her accent got really ghetto really quickly.

"Yes ma'am, but I would like to discuss the details of your case with you. Would you like to come in the office or would you like to discuss everything over the phone?" Leilani quickly said that we could speak over the phone because she was currently about to board a plane leaving Atlantic City.

She seemed real pleased about how this case should play out, but I told her I was never one to make any promises, but it was looking this was really an open and shut case. Before we got off of the phone she asked if we could have lunch when she got back to Atlanta, and I agreed.

Once hanging up the phone with Leilani, I quickly called Judge Mackey to call in my favor. She told me she had me and that I needed to quickly fax over the documents so that her secretary could file the proper documents.

**Emilio**

I had spent days inside of Leilani and I was actually a little tried, but she acted as if she couldn't get enough. Even as we rode the plane from Atlantic City to Atlanta, she asked if we could go to my private room and join the mile-high club. There was no way I was going to look as if I was going to tap out like a punk.

"I had a nice time Emilio. Thanks again," Leilani kissed me on the cheek once we got off of the plane.

She looked so cute on her tippy toes. She quickly walked her way over to her awaiting car got in. I swear the shorts she wore was so short and tight I was able to see everything that I had done inside her pussy.

My mind quickly snapped back into reality as I felt my phone vibrating in my pocket. When I took it out and looked at it, I saw it was Kelsey. I hadn't spoken to her in a few days so I knew I needed to answer the call.

"Hello Beautiful," I switched my voice making sure she wasn't able to hear how tried I was. As I was speaking I was getting in the back of the Maybach that was waiting to bring me to my Atlanta home.

"Hey, I hadn't heard from you in a few days, I got really worried." She sighed into the phone. She sounded so sexy when she worried. It was good knowing that I was on her mind because even though I fucked Leilani, Kelsey was in the back of my mind the entire time.

"I'm just getting back into town. I want to see you later. Are you busy tonight? I can pass by your house with a bottle of wine and some hot wings." I smiled to myself thinking about how much she loved hot wings and potato wedges.

I should have known she was going to ruin my day with her response because she took a deep breath. "I wouldn't mind you meeting you somewhere, but my home is a no go, King moved back in last night."

Laughing was the only thing I could do. Did she really try me like that? She was really serious about trying to make it work with this fuck nigga and he was fucking every bitch in the city of Atlanta.

"Yea ok Kels. Let me know, but I'll speak with you later." I tried to rush off of the phone with her, but she started to speak before I could.

"Don't be mad at me please Milo. You knew I was married from the beginning," she whined into the phone.

What she was saying was true, but that didn't take away from the way I felt. "Yea, you are right. I did know, but it's cool. My fault."

I hung up the phone faster than she could even process what I was saying. I could only blame myself because I was in love with a woman who belonged to someone else and it was up to me to do what I had to do in order to make her belong to me.

# Twelve

## King

"King I don't know why you take all of that from Kelsey any fucking way? She wasn't anyone before she met your ass. You made the bitch a famous lawyer," Chantae nagged as she sat across from me in the studio.

I knew she was in her feelings because I had told her the things that Kelsey had a problem with, but Kelsey was still my wife and she needed to be respected. "I know you are mad, but I bet not ever hear you call my wife a bitch. Chantae you were wrong for allowing Marri to stay up so fucking late. Her ass couldn't even function the next day."

"Yea, whatever King. I'm going to go. Mama said to call her." Chantae got up from the sofa and grabbed her purse. I didn't respond to her because she knew damn well I didn't want to speak to my mother. All she ever did was ask for money and act as if she had a big hand in raising me when she knew her damn self she just tossed us on our grandmother.

As soon as Tae left, I got a text from Leilani letting me know that had a doctor's appointment later and asked me if I wanted to come. I deleted the entire thread because she knew damn well I wasn't coming to the doctor's appointment.

After sitting at the mixing console, I dabbled with some ideas in my head for the mix tape, but shit wasn't coming together in my head, but then I got the idea to do a song for Kelsey. Either I was going to release it main stream or I was going to make it just for her.

"What's up Baby Girl," I answered the phone as soon as I heard it ring and it was Kelsey's face on the screen.

"Hey, uhmm I am about to pick up Kemarr from school, but afterwards I am going to the store to get something for dinner. Do you have a taste for anything special?" This was another thing I loved about my wife, her cooking was better than your mama's. When she cooked, she put her soul into it.

I had to think this one through really good because she ain't cooked for a nigga in a long time, so I wanted to make sure it was something that I truly had a taste for. "Lasagna. Bae make me some of your lasagna, please."

"Yea King, I got that for you. I'll see you when you get home." She spoke as dryly as she could as if I had just said something to piss her off.

"I love you Bae."

"Yea, love you too King." She again sounded dry as fuck, but then she hung up this time before I could say anything else.

With her being this mad at me I knew that I was going to have to apologize to her in front of the entire world. Which I wasn't scared to do. I wanted my wife back and I was going to do everything I fucking could to make sure I got her.

I played around with different sounds until I got a beat together that I could work with. It wasn't too slow where it sounded sad, but it was fast enough that she would be able to vibe too. Fast enough that everyone could jam to it.

The words flew into my brain so faster than I could get the ink on paper. I knew I wanted to talk about how much she was there for a nigga, how she cared for a nigga, and how she motivated a nigga. I felt that people needed to know that I was truly sorry for all the shit I did in my past and all the mistakes that I may accidentally make in the future.

When I felt that I had everything that I needed to make the song a smash hit, I decided to go home and chill with my family. Man I wanted to be a good family man, I really did because I knew that I had found gold.

Just as I was pulling into the drive way of my home, I get a phone call from Leilani. "What," I answered annoyed as fuck. I figured it was better to hurry and get this shit done and over with so that a nigga could move the fuck on with my life.

"Don't answer me no fucking what," she spat at me, but I ignored her attitude and asked her what the fuck she wanted yet again. "Papi, I need to talk to you about the baby. I think that we need to talk about where are going to live once the baby gets here."

She had to be completely delusional if she thought that I was going to leave my wife and live with her. "Bitch you know damn well it ain't no living together. Furthermore, that may not even be my baby. What happened to the money I gave you a few days ago? Why you ain't handle the sit then?"

"What the fuck was I going to do with seven-hundred dollars? I'm fucking Leilani, I don't need your money and I can't go to no cheap ass place anyways where anyone would see me. Then on top of that, you should be glad to be with me."

"Look Leilani let me go, but before I do let me tell you this shit. See that shit you pulled the other night in the club trying to hang with my wife, don't. I promise you I'm not the one to cross."

Leilani started laughing as if what I was telling her was a fucking joke, but she better remember who the hell she was talking too. "Kane stop it."

I pressed the button to end the call because I saw Kemarr opening the front door to the house and I knew it was only a matter of minutes before she was running out to me. It seemed like Leilani called back as soon as I hung up the phone.

"Daddy, come on, get out the car. I baked for you." Kemarr tried to open the car door, but it was locked. Once I turned off the car, I unlocked the door the door so she could open in.

"Hey Baby Girl," I gave her a kiss on her forehead. I quickly got out the car and locked the doors as Marri dragged me in the house by my hand.

"Daddy, come in. I made today special for you and Mommy ok? Mommy finished the food, but tonight I get to be the mommy waiter person and you two are on a date." She pulled me all the way inside. I laughed at how she seemed to have this all planned out.

When I got in the house, Kemarr brought me straight to the dining room. I thought Kelsey
would be in here, but she wasn't. I guess this was the time for my daughter to tell me the rules of the date because she started as soon as we were fully in the room.

"Daddy you have to be nice to my mommy so she can love you again. If you do what I tell you like pulling out her chair and telling her she's pretty, she'll love you as much as I do. Ok?" When pointed at me with her serious face. All I could do was laugh because I didn't know what to say. The fact that my marital issues were so bad that my child noticed bamboozled me.

"Yes ma'am. Marri where is your mommy?" I asked her as I walked into the kitchen and noticed my wife wasn't in there either.

"Oh her on the phone." Marri went over to the counter and started moving the cookies from the cookie sheet to a platter.

I nodded my head to my daughter's answer and decided to go upstairs and check on my wife. The night of her staying out late and then staying up to text was weighing my mind and I mind was telling me to make sure she didn't have another nigga on the phone.

The closer I got to our room, I listened for her, but I could barely hear her. It wasn't until I got into the room that I saw that she was on her side of the bed, facing the wall, on the phone whispering.

I was trying to listen, but she was speaking so low I couldn't hear shit, so I moved a little closer. Just as I was about to reach the foot of the bed, I tripped over the fucking rug. "Oh my gosh King, you scared me."

Kelsey jumped up from the bed and ended the call, walking over to me. "Who you was on the phone with?" I side eyed her. She looked at me and then rolled her eyes, slipping her phone in the back pocket of her jeans.

"Don't try and question me. You probably just getting home from some female. Niggas always want to make you look guilty and they are the ones doing the dirt. I wasn't talking to a nigga." She mumbled as she walked past me and out of the door.

To me, that's when she gave her own ass away. Never when I questioned her before did she ever mention the thought of another man. "Did I say you were talking to a nigga, but you must be the way you reacted to my question?"

My wife flicked her wrist at me as she moved down the stairs, but I was still on her heels. As soon as she reached the bottom step I got around her and pulled at her arm. "Kelsey, don't get fucked up. Because I swear on my granny I will fuck you and that nigga up."

She snatched her arm away from me and pushed me. "Man fuck you Kingston Taylor."

# Thirteen

## Leilani

Kane was playing with me and I knew he and I were destined to be together so I had to come up with a plan for him to end up leaving his wife. Little did his wife know, I hired a private investigator to
stalk her ass. That's just how I found of about Emilio Gustavo.

I figured that since this was her new love interest, I'd fuck him too, but also get him to claim his love for Kelsey in some sort of dramatic way that would lead back to Kane. Although I didn't have every little detail figured out, I knew my plan was going to work. I had even lit a candle every time I prayed.

"Lei, I know you not thinking about this man," my mother Reyna sat on side me on the chaise. Looking down, I noticed I had written Kane's name all over my page.

My mother knew everything there was to know about Kane, but she didn't care for him as much as I did nor did she understand the amount of love we shared for one another.

"Mommy, I didn't mean to. My brain just got the best of me." I laughed and started rubbing my stomach out of habit. "Kane and I are going to go look for homes when he gets back in town."

"That's nice, but didn't you tell me he was still legally married?" She folded her arms. My mother always knew how to ruin someone's day. I knew I should have never told her about him being married, but I didn't want her to find out from TMZ when we went public with our relationship.

I closed my book and got up from the chaise in order to get away from my mother. She had just ruined a peaceful day. "Leilani Marcella Rivera, I know you hear me. Isn't Kane still married? I see him on TV a lot and each time he is wearing a wedding band on his left hand."

"Mommy, I told you he is working on it. His wife is crazy. I told you she has ties to the mafia. She threatened to kill him. He has a daughter he can't just up in leave." I tried to explain to her, but she still had her arms folded as if she didn't want to hear what I was saying.

"Well he had eight more months to get his stuff together Lei. I just think you can do so much better." She walked over to the refrigerator and opened it. "Lei, why is there a bottle of vodka in the fridge?"

She was really starting to outstay her welcome and I was ready to send her back on the plane to California because she was going to damper my plans before they even were fully in motion.

"Mommy it's been in there since before I found out I was pregnant." I walked over to her and grabbed the bottle out of her hand, but she moved past me and went to empty it out in the sink. "Mommy why would you do that?"

She threw the empty bottle of Patron in the trash before she walked out of the kitchen.
"You are pregnant; you don't need it for one. Secondly, being drunk is a sin. Since you are already sleeping with a married man, you don't need to add any other sins to your life."

My mother continued her walk until she made it to her room and closed the door. "Bitch," I mumbled once she got out of ear range.

I quickly decided that I wanted to see Emilio. So I hit him up and let him know that my pussy was throbbing for him to be inside of me. Of course he replied with the quickness and hit me up telling me to meet him at the Four Seasons.

Getting to the hotel I went straight up to the room and knocked on the door. I was hoping her hurried it up because I wasn't trying to get seen by anyone, and people were already wondering who the fuck was the woman with big sunglasses and a hoodie.

"I see someone missed me," he opened the door with nothing on, but his dress slacks. He was too confident, but I mean he did have a reason to be. He was fine as fuck, and his dick was a monster, but at the end of the day he wasn't Kane.

I walked in and walked right past him. The room was a lot smaller than most of the rooms we get, but I'll take it. Usually we stayed in a suite, but I don't know what the hell happened today.

There was no need for us to do any talking, as soon as I sat on the bed Emilio was all over me. With his masculine hands rubbing on my body, he made me feel wanted and it was more intimate than it ever was with Kane. Emilio took his time was he kissed my lips while he slowly took off my shirt and unbuttoned my pants.

My head flew back when he started to massage my clit, causing chills down my spine. My juices were starting to flow and I was ready for him to stop teasing me with his fingers and give me his thick member. Trying to speed up the process, I undid his pants and slowly pulled them down.

Getting his nice thick and long shaft into my hand I opened my mouth and took in all of him. Moving my head up and down and moving my tongue around to massage him as well. Emilio placed his hand on the back of my head to guide me to how to please him, but I didn't need any help. I was a fucking pro at what I did.

After getting his to the point to damn near busting in my mouth, I pulled him out of my mouth and laid back down so that he could get on top on me and insert himself into my womanhood.

As Emilio entered his shaft into me, I tilted my head up to the sky because I felt the pleasure mixing with the pain from his size. I pictured that it was Kane inside of me instead of Milo, and the experience was as sweet as we made passionate love. The grunts and moans filled the air and heighted the experience.

"I need to ask you a question," I spoke up once we were done and I was putting my clothes back on to my body.

"What's up?" Emilio stood up from the bed and placed back on his dress slacks and boxers.

"You are into the Italian lifestyle, huh?" I was nervous about asking him the question, but it needed to be done and I knew that he was the one that would be able to do it. I just had to make sure to keep my tracks covered.

Emilio cut his eyes at me and glared at me for a few seconds. "What the fuck you just asked me, bitch?"

Rolling my eyes, I tried to push past the little name he called me. I knew I was going to have to watch what the fuck I said. "Emilio I know what you do, but I need a favor from you. I am willing to
pay whatever, but I need you to take my boyfriend's ex-wife out."

Emilio took a seat on the bed and started to play with his phone. I got up from the bed and walked over to stand in front of him. I was not to be ignored. "You can't hear me?"

He let out a slight laugh and continued to text unsaved number in his phone. I figured it had to be another bitch. Once he finished his message he stood up and walked into the bathroom. Emilio started to brush his teeth as if he didn't understand the words that were coming out of my mouth.

"Emilio, stop ignoring me. I asked you to perform a job. I have the money." I smacked my lips and threw myself down on the bed.

"No I'm not ignoring you. You don't understand the severity of the question you are asking me. Once this shit is done you can't take it back."

"I do understand and I just need your professional skills to make sure the job is done correctly," I nodded my shrugged my shoulders.

"I'm not doing that shit. And don't ask me again."

# Fourteen

## Kelsey

"Fuck King," I screamed as my husband rolled from off top of me. I'd be lying if I said he wasn't putting in work since he moved back into the house, but hell he better be trying to make up for lost time.

King let out a soft laugh, but I could tell that soon he would be fast asleep. His eyelids were heavy and he had positioned himself with his hands wrapped around my body. "I love you, and I'm forever sorry."

I just rubbed his arms, not knowing exactly how I should reply to what he was saying. My hurt was still there and the thoughts of the things King had done as well as the fight we got into was still in my head, but I knew that I wanted to make my marriage work, for myself and my family.

Soon the sounds of King's snore filled the room and the thoughts continued to fill my head, keeping me from my nap. Just as sleep started to consume my body, my phone started to ring.

"Hello," I hurried to answer my phone, trying not to wake my husband. "Hello, is someone there?" I asked the question after the moment of silence.

"Yea, hey Kelsey it's me, Leilani. I was wondering if you could meet me at the studio right now. I finally have those papers signed that you gave me. I wanted to give them to you so that way we can get started on my case."

After hearing her voice, I knew I wasn't going to sleep no time soon. I knew included in those stack of papers was a check with my name on it. "Yea, send me the address and I'll be there."

I hung up the phone with her once she told me she would send me the address to the studio and got out of the bed to take a shower and get dressed. I was moving slowly so I didn't wake up King because the last time he and I saw Leilani in the club, he had an attitude and told me she was just bad for business. Of course I had my thoughts as to why the hell my husband was so in his feelings about Leilani, but I knew the more I thought about it, the less likely I would be able to focus on getting my marriage back on track.

"Mommy, where are you going? I can go?" Kemarr ran out of her room as soon as she saw me pass her door. "Mommy, can I go?"

"Kemarr, Mommy is going to work. You are going to distract me." I rolled my eyes before I turned to face her. I felt bad that I didn't want my child to come, but once I saw her face, I gave in. "Fine, let's go get you dressed."

Went we back into her room and quickly found her an outfit to put on as I hurried to brush her hair into a bun. Kemarr talked the entire time it took for her to get ready to the very moment we arrived at the studio. She was making begin to regret my decision letting her come with me, but I knew she was my child and she was only five, so I let the feeling of annoyance leave my head.

"Kemarr, when we get inside and meet with Mommy's client, I need you to be on your best behavior and remain quiet, ok?" I opened the door for her spoke to her at the same time. Although my words and tone were soft, Kemarr knew not to embarrass me or it would be me and her when we got back to the car.

"Yes ma'am," was all she replied as I checked my phone to get the right studio number. When we walked into the room, it was pretty lit. Music was playing, people were sitting around, and Leilani was in the booth, singing her ass off.

I greeted the room, but I wasn't greeted with smiles from everyone. Dee, the producer that usually works with King looked as if my presence made him uncomfortable. "Aye Kels, if you here for that stuff for Kane, I'll be with you as soon as I finish with Lani."

"I don't need anything from you, I'm here for Leilani as well." I smiled at him and then turned my attention back to Kemarr who was tapping me on the back of my leg. "Marri, hold on please."

"But Mommy, I have something to tell you," she continued to tap on the back of my leg which was starting to bring the annoyed feeling back to my body.

"Kemarr Marie, I promise you that Mommy will talk to you as soon as we leave. Please stop hitting me. As a matter of fact, have a seat in the corner please." I pointed at the black sofa that rested on the wall.

I watched my child slowly stomp over to the sofa and sit down with a pout on her face, but she knew better than to fold her arms like she was mad at me. "Kelsey, I am glad you could come."

Hearing Leilani's voice so close to me threw me for a loop because I hadn't heard her come out the booth nor did I hear the music stop playing. "Hey, you have those papers?" I got straight to the point because I had my child with me.

"Hey Christina, can you go get that folder out of the car for me," Leilani called out to a girl whom I didn't know. She got up and did exactly what Leilani asked with no problems, hell I couldn't even get Kemarr to act that sweetly. "Well how is Kane doing?"

It wasn't unusual for people to ask me about my husband. I mean he was the hottest rapper out right now, so when she asked, I quickly replied that he was fine. "I know that's right, but I see you brought your daughter. She is so beautiful! She's how I want my child to look." "Thank you. I like to believe that she got her looks from me, but Kemarr come here and speak to Ms. Leilani."

Kemarr slowly got off of the sofa and came stood to my side. "I already know who she is."

"I know she's on TV, but now she's here in person Marri," I slightly laughed to cover up my child's rudeness.

Leilani seem to think Kemarr's remarks were cute. She greeted Kemarr with a hug, to which my child wasn't very receptive too. "Nice to meet you Kemarr, I'm Leilani."

Kemarr pushed Leilani off of her and I was damn sure ready to slap my child. "Why you acting like you don't know me. You that woman that be with my daddy. Didn't you come to my daddy's condo and when you left you were crying? Or that's not you?"

Leilani seemed to hear the words quicker than I did because she quickly tried to hug Kemarr, I guess in an effort to make it seem like my child was confused or something. One thing I knew I about my child was, she wasn't dumb.

"Oh my gosh honey you must've," Leilani patted the back of Kemarr's head. It seemed as if everything was going in slow motion because my anger was slowly building. I knew what the fuck it meant for Leilani to be coming to the condo, but it was bothering me that he had this bitch in my face.

Just before I was about to click out on everyone, the Christina bitch came back into the room with the folder. "Hey Christina you can just give it to her Kelsey, I think she's in the rush."

Leilani damn near ran over to Christina to get the folder from her. Kemarr looked up at me and looked for a reaction. "Nah, she good. I won't be accepting this case." I shook my head at her and grabbed Kemarr's hand.

My main goal was getting out of here without acting an ass if front of my child. No, Leilani didn't owe me any loyalty, but she knew I was married to King and her ass still came in my face. If Kemarr wasn't with me, I'm pretty sure that I would have fought Leilani and beat the fuck out of her at that.

As I was placing Kemarr in the back of my truck, I heard Dee running towards me. "Ayo, Kels let me holla at you."

I was upset with Dee's ass too because I am more than sure that he was just acting like that when I came in because he knew what the fuck was going on. Closing the door to where Kemarr was, opened up the passenger door in the front and reached over to turn the car on so that I could turn on the air.

"Dee, you don't owe me any explanations. I know you were trying to be loyal to your friend." I closed the door to my truck and turned to Dee.

He hung his head low and shook his head. "Man, Kane don't even fuck with that broad anymore. I just ain't wanna say anything when you walked in and caused any unnecessary drama."

There was nothing I could do, but laugh at sad this situation really was. "You know the funniest part is? The funny part is that my child, my five-year-old child, had my back more than y'all grown asses. Hell she ain't even know what was really going on, but she knew enough to know that Leilani didn't need to be in her father's home."

"Kels, mane I'm sorry yea." Dee just shrugged his shoulders. I knew he didn't have anything else to say because he knew his friend was wrong. Hell King knew that King was wrong.

I shook my head and just walked over to the driver's side of the car, opening my door to get in. "And next time you see me in a place with a bitch that you know my husband is fucking, just give me a heads up."

I finally got in my car, and started to drive off. I wasn't driving off mad because I didn't want to seem that emotionally unstable. My feelings were hurt, I can't lie. It seemed that King always found a

way to embarrass me.

"Mommy, are you mad at me? You seem a tad upset." Kemarr's soft voice rose over the low music that was playing through the speakers.

"No Baby girl, you did not do anything wrong. Mommy is just having a moment, ok?" I looked at her through the rearview mirror and I saw how sad she looked, and that pissed me off even more.

King was so fucking selfish that he brought my child into this. My child knew who this bitch was, and that was in no way acceptable.

Once we got to the house, my blood was literally boiling and I was feeling the sweat begin to run down my back. He had me more than fuck up, and I was just about to show him who the fuck he was playing with.

After I made my child something to eat and set her up in the movie theater, making sure that she would be entertained for a while, I scurried upstairs to pack Kemarr and I a bag. I made sure to pack enough stuff to make sure we would be ok for at least a week. Once they were in the car, and I made sure to keep some shoes and a coat by the door, I headed back into the kitchen. I started to fix his favorited breakfast foods because I knew he hadn't eaten today. Grits, bacon, sausage, and waffles was all I fixed.

I made my way back upstairs and headed to my closet. Stripping out of my professional clothing and slipped into something very revealing. A blush pink lace teddy that rested so pretty on my caramel brown skin. I took a peek in the mirror and made sure that everything was in place. Hair, make-up, and body.

"Baby, wake up." I walked over to the bed and placed soft kissed all over my husband's body. I slowly placed my left hand under the cover and began to play with his tool. As I felt it harden in my hand, King slowly awoken. "Come down stairs, I made you something to eat."

King let out a loud yawn and got out of the bed, smacking me on my ass as he followed me down stairs. "Where is Marri? You ain't got on these sexy ass clothes."

"She's entertained, just worry about me right now."

"Damn, all this shit for me," King asked me as I turned the fire down on the pot of grits and turned the fired off under the skillet that I had just fixed the bacon in. "You know how to treat your man."

Since King wasn't facing my, I rolled my eyes and bit my lip. Little did he know what I had in store for his no good ass. I was sick and tired of having him walk all over me like I was just a piece of trash.

Once the plate was done, I turned to my husband and wrapped my arms around his neck. "Why don't you go have a seat at the table and let me bring the food to you," I seductively demanded. King gave me a kiss on my lips and headed to the table.

"You know, I love what we have going on. I am so happy that we can get past the bullshit, you know. Like I fucking love you Kelsey, you and Kemarr. I just want us to be a good family unit." King sat at the table, laid back in the chair like some thug with his legs open and one arm resting on the table, just watching me.

As mad as I was, I continued to play along, so I continued to nod my head and smile. I grabbed a wine glass out of the cabinet and a bottle of juice apple out of the refrigerator. After fixing him a glass, I brought it to him, then I brought him his food.

"Thank you Baby," King started to tear into his food as soon as it hit the table. "Baby, come sit on my lap and eat with me."

"Hold on baby, let me fix myself a plate," I flashed him a smile. I damn sure wasn't about to sit on his lap.

When I walked back to the stove, I took the spoon out of the pot of grits and grabbed it in one hand and grabbed the skillet in the other had. I waited a few seconds to make sure that King wasn't watching me. When I looked over, his face was right in his plate.

I don't know where my strength came from, but I was able to carry the big ass pot and skillet at once. I sat the skillet on the island closest to the table and used both of my hands to grip the handles of the pot of grits. "Aye, baby can you make me a pot of coffee please?"

"Fuck," I mumbled to myself and moved everything back over to the stove. "Yea babe, sure." I walked over to the Keurig and turned it on after I switched out the cups.

The longer I thought about the hurt that King had been putting me through the faster I wanted to get this shit done and over with. I loved my husband, my entire life my mother taught me that I was supposed to cater to my husband and my life would be smooth sailing. I did as I was taught, and testy waters in this damn relationship are worse than Hurricane Katrina.

Once the coffee was done, I grabbed the cup of steaming hot coffee and walked over to my husband. He was unexpectedly waiting for the cup of hazelnut flavored coffee. The closer I got the more my hand started to shake. I was twitching to give this to him.

Finally, I was standing right beside him, but he never looked my way, waiting for me to sit the cup down on the table, but I didn't. I took the hot beverage and poured it on top of his head. "Bitch," he roared.

"You had that fucking bitch in my face and you knew you were fucking her! Fuck you Kingston, I'm done with you and this marriage." I took off towards to where I left my coat and shoes, and hurried to put them on.

I felt like I wasn't moving fast enough because as soon as I ran into the hallway to get Kemarr from the theater, King caught me and slammed me against the wall. His breathing was heavy, but his face was red and I knew the coffee had to burn him badly. His large hand was wrapped around my throat, but not tight enough to the point where I couldn't breathe, but it was tight enough that I couldn't move.

"Kelsey, what the fuck is wrong with you?" King let go of be, but punched the wall right next to my head. "I swear, you be fucking playing with me. Who the fuck told I was fucking Leilani?"

The fact that he knew what and who I was talking about only added more fire to my furry. "Oh so you know who the fuck I'm talking about huh? Man King, I'm sick of you. I'm leaving. Kemarr and I are gone."

"Kemarr honey, let's go." I walked in the theater and turned off the movie in the middle of her watching it. Kemarr looked from me to her father and slowly removed the blanket from her lap and stood up.

King snatched the remote from my hand and turned the movie back on. "Kemarr have a seat baby girl. You can leave Kelsey, but my child isn't going out the house on a school night."

Kemarr was confused and she didn't know what to do. She started to sit back down, but she was leaving with me whether King liked it or not. I walked over to her and picked her up and started to walk towards the door, but King blocked my exit.

"Move Kingston," I tried pushing him, but it was to no avail. King didn't budge instead he folded his arms. He knew that I was no match to his six-nine, muscular body frame.

I looked up at him and he looked back down at me, and laughed. "You think I'ma let you take my daughter from me? You leaving because a bitch told you I fucked her? I ain't want that bitch, I want you. I want our family."

My mind was running wild and my emotions were all over the place. Kemarr began to cry so I knew the conversation King and I were having needed to stop. "King, just let us go please. She's crying." Before I knew it, I had tears rolling down my cheeks as well. My life was so fucked up and I needed to get myself together for myself and my child.

King grabbed me by my arm and applied pressure. "You aren't leaving me Kelsey. We gotta talk about this. I will not lose you." He got right in my face, but I didn't know how to feel about his statement. Did he tell me that because he loved me or was it a threat?

"Daddy, let Mommy go please. You are hurting her," Kemarr reached over to try and remove her father's hand from my arm. The sound of her voice cracking killed me inside and I prayed her cries were enough for King to stop.

For a few more seconds we all stood there in silence before King let go of me and stepped out of the way for Kemarr and I to leave. I walked as fast as I could to my car. Once Kemarr was in the backseat and buckled, I got in myself and started the car.

Panic started to set in when I saw King running out the house towards us. I started the car and threw it into drive. As I drove down the busy streets of Atlanta, I looked into my rearview mirror at my child. She sat in her booster seat with her head down, twirling her thumbs and sniffling her tears.

In that moment I didn't know what to do, didn't know what to say or even how to say it. I felt like I had failed her as a mother, as a woman. She didn't need to see her father and I act a fool because he didn't know how to act.

# Fifteen

## Kelsey

"So when are you going to answer his phone calls," Harmonie handed Kemarr her snack as the three of us sat in her kitchen. Since I left King damn near two weeks ago, Kemarr and I have been staying over here.

"Marri, go watch TV in the living room please?" I waited for my child to get up and exit the room before I started to speak. "Monie, you don't understand how I feel. He didn't deny the fact that he fucked her. He thinks she told me, but she didn't Kemarr told me. You don't understand how it feels for your own child to know your husband is cheating on you before you do."

My mind was replaying the little scene from the studio over and over in my head, and each time I got more and more upset. Since I had been here, King had called nonstop, texted a ton, and even been in my DM's on my social media accounts, but none of it was working because I was tired of it. I'd even blocked and reported his pages and our pictures.

This was never supposed to be my life, and I hated it. Emilio had even started acting funny, but I couldn't even focus on that. Between Kemarr asking a million questions and me just not being able to concentrate on anything much; I had to tell my job that I wouldn't be taking any cases for a few weeks.

"Look, I may not be married or have any kids of my own, but I know you shouldn't have to go through this with someone who is supposed to love you." She was right. My husband wasn't supposed to treat me like this, but for some reason I miss him.

I couldn't help it. My husband was all I knew, no matter what. The memories they we have created still linger in my heart. I want the man I first met. The man who thought I was the best thing since sliced bread. Somewhere in my heart I do believe that the real Kingston was still inside Yung Kane.

I played around with the straw in my cup of orange juice, trying to decide what I was going to say in response of what my best friend said. "I know Monie. I didn't mean anything persona by that. I just don't think you truly understand how I feel."

Harmonie let out a slight laugher a began to pull away from the table, shaking her hand. "You do whatever you want Kels." She headed out the kitchen, still laughing to herself. I didn't understand why she was so mad at me.

After she left, I decided to go in the living room and check on my child. I felt so bad for her because I knew that her life was being flipped upside down and she didn't understand why. I never wanted her to grow up without having both of her parents living with her. I've officially failed as a parent.

Kemarr was sitting on the sofa, playing with her Barbie dolls. God had blessed me with a beautiful daughter and she was wiser than she was supposed to be at her age. "Mommy, can I talk to Daddy please?"

She threw her doll die and patted the area on side of her on the sofa for me to sit down. Kemarr was such a little woman and I loved it. Once I took my seat next to her, I pulled her in close because her warmth always eased my heavy heart. "You know Daddy and I love you right? No matter what, we love you more than any and everything."

"I know that already. I'm you guys' only child, silly." She cracked her own self up with her more than confident response. "I just haven't spoken to him in such a long time. I was hoping he would come get me for some ice cream."

As much as I wanted to be an ignorant ass hoodrat baby mama and tell my child she didn't need to speak to her dumb ass daddy, I couldn't be like that. I took my phone out of my back pocket and handed it to her. She unlocked the iPhone with her thumb print and proceeded to dial her father's number from heart.

It seemed as though King wasn't going to answer, but right before she was about to hang up, he picked up. His voice wasn't loud enough for me to hear, but the conversation seemed to be going well from the excitement in my child's voice.

Though my husband wasn't perfect, he still did have some good qualities as a father and I didn't want to take that from him. The look of overjoy that was plastered across my child's face was more than enough for me to give him his props for being a father instead of just a baby daddy.

Soon the conversation was over and Kemarr threw the phone back at me and hopped off of the sofa, cheering. "Mommy, Daddy said he's going to pick me up in one hour, and I'm spending the night. We are going to the movies Mommy. He said you are welcome to come with us."

King knew damn well I wasn't going to be going anywhere with them. "How does he know where we are?" I had listened to the entire conversation and she didn't mention us being at her godmother's home nor did I tell King where we were.

"He said that he was just going to track your phone or something, but Mommy are you coming with us?"

"Mommy is going to sit this one out Marri so that way you and your father can have you all's date alone. Is that fine," whether she agreed or not she didn't have much of a choice. About the tracking thing, I couldn't even get mad at it. We both were still sharing our locations with each other and that had totally slipped my mind.

Kemarr shrugged her shoulders as if it really didn't matter to her either way. Hell all she knew was that with Daddy she got whatever she wanted. "Come on Kemarr, let's get you ready and pack a bag so you can go."

Trying to get an active five-year-old ready was hard work. Especially when the five-year-old was overly fabulous like her mother. Giving her a bath, combing her hair, dressing her, and packing her an overnight bag was like a job.

Kemarr was running all across the room that she and I were sharing. Since I had to buy stuff to sustain us until we either went back home or got our own place, the room was covered with shopping bags, but my child made sure to rip them apart looking for a specific outfit. Not to mention King showed up in thirty minutes and not an hour. Thankfully Monie let him in and he sat in the living room.

Just knowing he was in the house with us made me nervous. I wasn't scared of him or anything, but I was still nervous. Anyone would probably feel some type of way if their husband was in the same place as them, but things were so bad that they weren't even speaking.

My heart was beating rapidly and my hands begin to shake. As I placed the last of Kemarr's items into the glittery pink suitcase that she cried over when we were in the store, I felt myself being giddy like a little ass high school girl.

Once I was done everything, I handed Kemarr her bag and told her that she could leave after giving her a big hug and a kiss. She flew out of the room and into the living room. I could hear her scream with glee for her father. Once things got quieter, I figured they had left so I started to strip out of my clothes to get into the shower.

When I stood up from bending down to take my panties off, I heard the door opening. Naturally, I hurried to cover my body with my hands to shield my lady parts. To my surprise, it was King standing in the doorway.

The initial shock worn off, but hatred filled my heart. Most times I would be overcome with the sensation of lust to see my husband standing before me in a pair of basketball shorts that allowed the imprint of his massive dick to show, but not today.

"I was just coming to speak and say that we were about to go. I'll bring her back tomorrow or whenever you want her home." He spoke as if he was nervous too. As if he was looking for the proper words to say so that I wouldn't be even more upset than I already was.

I didn't want to talk to him, so I just nodded my head and looked at the door him hand was resting on, wondering when he would leave. He lingered for a few more seconds, staring at my face and not my body which made me wonder what was on his mind, "No matter what, and if I'm lying God could strike me dead right now, I love you more than anything. My father fucked up my mentality and I didn't see anything that wrong with my actions, but I promise I'm going to start going to counseling with the pastor to get myself right for you, for Kemarr, for myself. Look Kelsey a nigga ain't trying to lose his family."

Kemarr coming to rush him was the only thing that caused King to leave the room. I just sat down on the bed and let the tears flow. Why was it that this man had done me so wrong, but yet I was still in love with him? King was the love of my life, but yet he drags me through hell and back, but I still loved him with my entire being. I guess I'm just a typical bitch.

# Sixteen

## Harmonie

"Kelsey what the fuck is wrong with you? Get the hell up, bitch we are going out!" I busted into her room and this bitch was sitting on her bed, wrapped in a towel, crying. King had left the house all of three hours ago and here she was crying, still. I loved my girl, but crying over a nigga was not what we were about to do.

She rolled over in the bed so that she wasn't facing me. Kelsey should have known that I was a petty bitch. Walking around the bed so that we would be face to face was nothing for me to do. "Harmonie I don't want to go out," she whined.

"I didn't ask you if you wanted to; I said that you were going. Now get your ass up. I'll pick you out something to wear out of one of these million bags you have on the floor." Kelsey had spent at least twenty-thousand dollars on clothes for her and Kemarr. Of course everything had a name of them and most of the shoes had red soles, but that was just who Kelsey was.

The sparkly purple caught my eye, causing me to want to see what was inside of it. A black cotton, strapless, bodycon dress was the first thing I pulled out, followed by a couple blouses. I decided that the dress was good enough. My friend was fine as hell so I knew the dress would be beautiful on her. Especially with her hair, makeup, and jewelry. After roaming through some Louboutin bags, I found a strappy pair of silver red bottoms. Her outfit was complete.

I set out her entire outfit at the foot of her bed, but Kelsey still hadn't budged in the time it took me to get everything together. The clock on the cable box said 10:30 pm and I knew that we needed to leave the house in an hour in order to make it to the club for twelve.

"Kels, hurry and do your face and hair. We have to leave the house in about an hour so I'm about to get myself together," I spoke over my shoulder while I was on my way out of the door to her room.

Tonight was going to be good for the both of us because I had been going through my own relationship drama as well, and as much I want to so badly tell my best friend what's going on in my life, I know that my drama doesn't even compare.

Being fine was exactly what Kelsey and I were going to be. I'd just bought a black dress with a lace cut outs. I knew to pair it with some black strappy heel sandals. I don't go to play with these hoes. I went to slay, bitch.

About forty-five minutes later, my best friend entered my room looking just as stunning as ever. Hopefully she got snatched up by some fine ass man at the club who would give her that work and make her forget about her wack ass husband. The world loved him, but if they knew how he really was, I swear they'd think twice.

Kelsey looked down at herself, making sure she was ok since I was just staring at her. "Is something on my dress," she tried to durst off the imaginary crumbs.

"No Kelsey. You just look stunning! I mean that shape is everything. The titts are sitting oh so pretty!" I turned away from her to finish the finishing touches on my make-up. My hair was done and I was fully dressed, but I wanted to make sure that my highlight was poppin'.

Kelsey walked over to my vanity counter and folded her arms. "Bitch who the fuck is you trying to sleep with tonight with that dress on? Well that piece of a dress on."

Adorning us in the mirror, we were stunning and I would have to be us if we weren't us. I was on the slimmer side, but my hips were just as pronounced as Kelsey's. "No, we need to worry about who the fuck you are sleeping with tonight."

Kelsey playfully pushed me from my response, but I was being so serious and she knew I was. She was my girl and I just wanted the best for her ass.

Arriving at Club Lyve, the line was around the corner, but thankfully we wouldn't have to wait. Hell, that was one of the advantages of Kelsey being with King's duck ass. The body guard spotted us getting to the Uber and came to help us out.

Women and men in the line were trying to see who we were, but they would be disappointed to see it was little ole us getting out of the car. The bodyguard must have noticed too because he commented on it. "All this attention you all are getting is like Kane himself is in that car."

Kelsey did a sly laugh, but continued to push forward. Once inside the club, the shit was poppin'. The strobe lights were flashing everywhere and the music was banging. The bodyguard lead us to a section by the stage, and I was ready to start ordering the bottles.

Every bitch in there was trying to land her a baller because everyone who was somebody in the city of Atlanta was in Lyve on a Saturday night. Local rappers and artists who were known around the world were in this bitch. Even Trey Songz posted on Snap that he would be in the building tonight, now that was someone I wouldn't mind going home with.

Just as we got settled and have placed our orders, I noticed my lil boo thang walking our way. Fine as all of heaven was the best way to describe him. Six-three, a solid two hundred pounds of muscle, a slight beard, with a nice ass man bun that let his curl pattern show. He was the finest light skin nigga that I had ever saw, and the fact that he was in the streets made my panties wet.

Kelsey didn't know who the fuck he was, but the closer he got the more paranoid she got. "Harmonie why didn't you tell me you were coming tonight," he stepped up into the section and placed a kiss on my forehead before extending his hand out to Kelsey. "Nice to meet you. I'm Sevyn Matthews; owner of this club and Harmonie's soon to be boyfriend."

I tried to turn my head away from Kelsey because I knew that she was totally aggravated at what he'd just said. Yes, I was talking to someone and didn't tell her, but I had my reasons. It wasn't like I was just going to not tell her; I just wanted to wait until her life was better first. She didn't need my drama and her drama at the same damn time.

"Crazy that you are about to be her boyfriend and I have never heard anything about you, but hello my name is Kelsey," she reached to shake his hand. Sevyn laughed off her shade and sat down next to me.

He complimented how beautiful I looked tonight, but it was going to take a lot more than a couple nice words for me to just be able to get over what he'd done. "Can I come over tonight?"

I looked at him and started to laugh. He knew what he was doing because he knew that his dick was the best thing I had ever discovered.

Pushing my hair behind my ear, he leaned in and licked it. Trying to control myself, I decided to rub my hands against my thighs. Sevyn began to lick down to my neck and plant small, wet, kisses. This nigga was trying to fuck me in the middle of the club. "Stop," I finally moaned.

Sevyn took his tongue away from my neck and stood up from the sofa. "I'll be over after I close this place up. Nice meeting you Kelsey," he waved at her and then left the section.

My best friend couldn't wait for the man to get far enough before she turned to me and started to go in. "After all the shit we have been though Harmonie Brooks, how dare you get into a relationship and try not to tell me? I am your best friend. We are supposed to tell each other everything, why the fuck didn't I know?"

Right before I could answer, the waitress had finally arrived with our bottles. Of course they had the little sparkler attached to them, but I was hoping the flames would hurry and die. The waitress poured Kelsey and I both glasses of the Ciroc and mixed them for us. I took a sip of my glass before I responded. "Kelsey you are my best friend, but you have a lot going on in your life right now. I am not about to just throw my shit at you until we figure out how to handle the drama going on in your life."

Kelsey folded her arms trying to analyze what I had told her without automatically saying I was right. I knew I was right so rather she told me or not, I was fine with what I had said. Never would I try to just play my best friend.

The music in the club started blaring and "No Problem" by Chance The Rapper started to come through the speakers. Finally, it was time for us to turn up. Both Kelsey and I started vibin' off the music with our drinks in our hands. This was our song! Hell I wished a bitch would start some shit so they could see just who the fuck we were.

Two hours and two bottles later, we were on our asses. Our section had filled up pretty quick as more celebrities came into the building, they spotted Kels and just welcomed themselves. I didn't say anything because they had bottles and weed, so they were cool with me. A few minutes ago I spotted Leilani walking around the club; I should have known then that the night was only going to get worse from there.

Not wanting to mess up Kelsey's high, I decided that I was going to keep my little sighting of the home-wrecker to myself. Hell, I was quite high myself. There were so many blunts in rotation, and I had to put my lips on every one of them.

Our section was so lit that bitches were dancing on tables shaking their asses as if this was Magic City, and niggas were throwing dollars like they were Mardi Gras beads. This was truly what I needed to get my mind right. Shit with Sevyn was getting deeper, and he was starting to show me who he really was. I was stuck between falling for this nigga or just tucking my tail between my legs and moving on.

Yea I had money of my own, but this nigga shitted dough. He owned the hottest club in the city of Atlanta, the most poppin' chain of five-dollar carwashes, and this nigga was moving weight. Sevyn was that nigga in the streets and with me being on his arm, that made me that boss bitch. I'd always wondered how Kelsey felt being with someone of power, but now I was about to get my chance to find out.

"Milo," I heard Kelsey scream as she ran past me and over to her ex-lover. I watched as her drunk ass threw herself into his arms, but I didn't like the reaction he'd given her. Although he did catch her, he seemed surprised, like he'd been caught or something. I stood there in a trance watching the entire thing, waiting to see what the fuck he felt surprised about.

Because Kelsey was drunk, she was more than horny and was damn near trying to fuck this man in the middle of all these people. Emilio started to relax after he checked his surroundings, and he started to be more receptive to her embrace. I was so busy in their business I never realized Sevyn had come back. "Stop being nosey," he spoke as he slapped my ass.

After the instant shock wore off, I turned around and hit him in his shoulder. I was used to my ass being slapped, but he put way too much force behind that. "That's my best friend. I'm just minding our business."

Sevyn laughed and pulled me closer to him as they played "Do You Mind" by DJ Khaled. I guess they were about to slow down the mood to give people a moment to rest. We swayed to the music, and it felt good. I hadn't been with a man in a long time. This was a good feeling to be with someone again. There was nothing like a man's touch.

I'd almost forgotten we were in the middle of the club since Sevyn and I were staring so deep into each other's eyes, but the yelling my best friend was doing made me remember. "You in the club with this bitch?"

When I turned around I saw Kelsey in Emilio's face with Leilani standing right next to him. I couldn't get over there fast enough because Leilani swung her fist and it landed on the side of Kelsey's head. Before I could help, Kelsey grabbed Leilani by her neck and started swinging. She was getting her and Emilio was trying to get Kelsey to stop, but with the mixture of alcohol, weed, and pain she had going on in her body, she was taking every last frustration out on Leilani's face.

There was no reason for me to jump in a fair fight, until one Leilani's little friend's decided her best friend had enough of getting her ass beat. "Bitch you tried it," I went after the raggedy bitch with my fists already cocked. I almost felt bad for this heffa because she couldn't fight, but I had to teach her a lesson about trying to jump in other people's fights.

Just as I was getting tired, a bunch of security guards came and broke up both fights. I looked in amazement as the bitch I was fighting was holding her nose, still trying to talk shit, but Leilani was damn near unrecognizable. She had blood in her hair and all over the bright ass yellow dress she had decided to wear.

Searching for my best friend, I didn't see her. Hell I didn't see Emilio either. The people in the club all stood around waiting to see what else was going to happen now since the lights had got turned on and the music stopped. "What the fuck are y'all looking at? Put them cameras up before I beat y'all asses too." I screamed at the bystanders who were trying to get their snap stories lit for the night.

"Stop making a damn fool of yourself," Sevyn grabbed me by my arm and lead me away from the crowd. I mugged every bitch on the way there. "You good?" Sevyn asked when we got to his office.

He threw me onto the sofa and closed and locked the door. "No I'm not good. I don't know where my best friend is and she just got into a fight."

"She's with my potna' Emilio, she's good."

# Seventeen

## Kelsey

"Take me home," I screamed as Emilio sped down the interstate going a place that was a mystery to me. My anger was making me shake and I just started to swing on Emilio. How could he hurt me too? Then it was with the same bitch that my husband had slept with as well. It was like this bitch was a ghost who wouldn't stop hunting me.

Emilio blocked most of my punches, but the one that went to his right eye caused him to swerve into oncoming traffic. The bright head lights blinded me, but I was ready to die. I didn't give a fuck and no one else did either obviously. Milo saved us when he spent the wheel in the opposite direction and landed us on the shoulder of the interstate.

The panic wore off and I let out a breath that I hadn't realized I was holding. I knew was my life was about to be over, but when it didn't come true I felt stupid for neglecting to forget about Kemarr. I threw my head into my lap to regain control of myself and the tears just begin to fall. Loving a nigga was what fucked me over, and if that wasn't as basic as it came, I didn't know what was.

I felt Emilio watching me, but when he started to rub my back, I let of a loud sob. Yet in still after all of this, I had so much love for Emilio and I hated it. He was supposed to be my knight in shining armor, but he was fucking a demon.

Emilio placed the car into drive and took back off towards our destination. I must've fallen asleep because I woke up to Emilio tapping me on my thigh. I picked my head up and noticed that two valet attendants were coming towards the car. "I left all my shit in the club," I stressed to Milo, but he didn't respond to me. He only just got out of the car when the attendants opened our doors.

Feeling played, I got out the car and followed him into the lobby of the hotel. We were greeted by the staff, which was crazy since it was three in the morning. I got a chance to read one of their shirt's and I realized we were at the St. Regis. At least I knew my location, even if I couldn't call anyone to tell them where the fuck I was.

Once we got to the room, Emilio still didn't talk to me. He went into the bathroom leaving me all alone in this big ass room. I sat in the chair next to the window because I was didn't know if he'd fucked the bitch in the bed or not.

The room was filled with Emilio's things like he'd been living there. All the money this man had, he was choosing to live out a basic ass hotel room in a luxury hotel. At least he wasn't junky because off of his shit was neatly placed. Even the phone charger that was resting on the nightstand, in a circle like you'd do a cable wire.

"You can sit on the bed. I ain't fuck her in here," Milo mumbled as he came back into the room and threw a set of towels in my lap. I watched him walk over to the closet and pull out a white muscle shirt. He brought it over to me and placed it in my lap.

He really was acting cold towards me and I had no idea why. I had never done anything personal to him. If anything, I should be the one who was upset because of how he did me back then and now. I didn't let it worry me because I wanted to shower more than anything. I wanted to feel the hot water beat against my skin and I needed it to relax my tense muscles.

Inside of the bathroom I started to undress and got a chance to finally look in the mirror to see what damage did the fight do to me. The side of my face that Leilani hit was swollen, and I knew that by morning I was going to have a bruise, but I was ok with it because I knew Leilani would look worse.

Getting in the shower, I realized that more of my body was hit than I thought because my muscles were so tight. The entire time I prayed to God that He would grant me freedom from my pain and allow me to be a better role model for my child.

When I got back into the room, Milo was standing in front of the mirror on the phone. I figured he had to be handling business because the way he was speaking and acting now was exactly how he used to act when we were together and he was in the streets.

He must've heard me enter the room because he turned around and looked at me. We shared a quick glance, but I broke the stare-off after a couple of seconds when I looked at the bed. Milo make some sort a grunt and walked past me, heading to the bathroom. After I heard the door close, I rolled my eyes and decided to get in the bed.

I pulled back the comforter and the flat sheet to make sure I didn't see any hair or any strange stains. Once I satisfied my concerns, I slid into the right side of the bed and grabbed the remote to turn on the flat screen which was mounted to the cream colored wall.

Milo coming back into the room with his body still wet and nothing, but a towel wrapped around his waist distracted me from the movie that I had been all into just a few seconds earlier. This man was like a Greek god or something with his tall stance and muscular body. He had the most beautiful head of hair that I'd ever seen on a man, it was naturally jet black. His copper tone made it looked like he had diamonds or glitter on his body.

No way was I going to allow him to notice how much I was feeling him in that moment. I didn't know if it was the weed and alcohol I'd put in my system or what, but my clit was jumping at this nigga. Just as I heard the towel drop to the floor, I maintained my focus on the lame ass horror movie.

My mind began to wonder and hope at the fact that I knew that Milo was about to slip into his Calvin Klein underwear, leaving his dick print on full display. Yet at the same time, I still felt hurt by tonight and I knew I wanted to talk to him. I waited until I heard the closet door closed and then I finally looked.

Just like I knew, he was wearing those Calvin Klein underwear, grey. His thick, long member was on full display and I knew I needed to look away before I did something I shouldn't. Emilio came over to the bed and sat on the edge of it and grabbed the bottle of Jergens off of the nightstand and started to lotion his body.

Although I didn't know the right words to say, I just started the conversation. "Emilio, I know we aren't together, but I just wanted to tell you that I am hurt by tonight," I started to speak.

"Man what the fuck do you want for me huh? You mad because I was with another bitch? Kelsey, it is no secret that I love you, but how is it fair to me that you can bounce around from me to your husband? You use me to make you feel better after he's fucked every bitch in the street."

Emilio threw himself from the bed in a rage and onto his feet as he spoke so passionately. Hell, I didn't know that he still loved me that much, but it did make me feel better.

"I'm not with King anymore because of her. That same bitch you are fucking is the same bitch that fucked my husband, and it hurt like hell tonight to see not only did she get my husband, but she got the true love of my life. My marriage is over, but it was a shame for the beginning, but I can't lose you Emilio. Not again, I can't." My voice began to change as the tears begin to form in my eyes. I couldn't believe that I was finally admitting how I felt.

Milo didn't respond to me, but he walked over to me and pulled me close to him. He wrapped his arms around my waist and held me close to his chest and allowed my tears to continue to fall. "You aren't going to lose me, Kels. If you promise me that your marriage is over, I'll be yours forever."

"You promise," I wiped my face with the back of my hand. Emilio kissed the crown on my head and started to gently rub my back. He made me feel at ease.

"I promise."

# Eighteen

## King

"Kemarr, keep playing. I gotta take this," I waved my phone at her so she saw that I had an incoming call. She nodded her head and continued to insert her tokens into the SpongeBob game we were hogging in Chuck-E-Cheese.

Kemarr and I were having so much fun together that I didn't want to give her back. I texted my Kelsey to let her know that I'd just bring Kemarr to school on Monday and she can get her from there. I wished it could've been a family thing, but I could understand why it wasn't.

My phone was still vibrating in my hand, so I answered Leilani's call. "What's good?" There was no way Leilani and I would ever be what she wanted, but if she was truly carrying my child, I knew I needed to man up.

All I could hear was her sniffling into the phone, and I began to worry that something was wrong with the baby. "Leilani what is wrong? The baby good?"

"Your crazy wife jumped me with her friend and now I am in the hospital. I told you she wasn't any good for you, Kane. She tried to kill our child,"

"What the fuck you mean she jumped you Lani? Why would she jump you? That doesn't even sound like Kelsey," I headed towards the table and took a seat. People were all trying to size me up and see if it was really me, but being damn near seven-feet tall, it wasn't hard to tell.

Pulling my hood further on to my head, I sunk into my seat and waited for Leilani to explain to me why the fuck would my wife jump her. I know that Kelsey knows about the affair, but she ain't the type of woman to just go around beating up a bitch.

Leilani continued to cry into the phone, still not explaining to me what happened. "She was just angry at me. She just started swinging one me at the club with her little friend."

This heffa had to be lying to me. I know damn well she wasn't in anyone's club while pregnant with my child. "Why were you in the club?"

"That doesn't matter. Just come quick because I am worried about the baby," she cried into the phone. I told her to send me the address and that I would be on my way and just hung up the phone.

Calling Kelsey was the first thing I decided to do because I needed to get to the bottom of this, but her phone went straight to voicemail; so I called again. For the second time Kelsey's phone went straight to voicemail so I left her ass a message.

My life was really starting to get the best of me, and the only thing I had was my music. "Daddy, you think you could get me more tokens?" Kemarr's voice snapped me out of my feelings.

She was toting around a bundle of tickets and an empty cup. Once she emptied arm full of tickets on to the table, she sat down on the opposite side of the booth and picked up a slice of pizza and stuffed it in her mouth. My child was beautiful and I couldn't stop staring at her. With everything going on, she still had a smile on her face. Kemarr didn't have a care in the world. Her only concerns right now was what was she going to get, and I wanted to keep it that way.

"Kemarr, didn't I just spend a hundred dollars on tokens like an hour ago? Where are they?" I sat back up in my seat and watched her continue to eat her pizza in excitement.

"In the machines, silly. Man these games are addicting. You put in a token and you get tickets. The tickets get you stuff at the counter."

"Well we are going to have to come back because after you finish your pizza, we are going to cash in your tickets and it is time for us to leave."

Of course Kemarr wasn't too happy about that, but she didn't have much of a choice. I'm happy I didn't get her any more damn tokens because this child had five thousand tickets. She ended up with a Chuck-E doll and a hell of a lot of candy. The entire ride to the hospital all she did was smack her gums.

I didn't know how to explain to Kemarr why we were there. I knew she was bound to ask because she always asked a million and six questions. I figured I was just going to ignore her until she shut-up.

The air inside of the hospital was thin. I've always disliked hospitals, mainly because of the smell. They wreak of death and not to mention how depressing the white paint and bright lights were. I waited for Kemarr's questions to start, but they never did. I had to turn around to make sure that she was still following me off of the elevator. I knew that if something had happened to her, her mother would've killed me because I wasn't holding her hand. When I looked, she was right behind me, with her iPad in her hand. From the looks of it she was on some game or some drawing app, since that was all she ever did.

Satisfied with my child being close enough for comfort, I turned my attention back to the receptionist desk that I was walking up on. The older lady behind the desk looked as if she took her job very seriously. She had three computer screens and her classes were sitting on the tip of nose, and still her face was in the monitor. "I'll be with you in one second, Sir." She continued to beat her keys and not make eye contact.

This lady took three minutes before she finally got to me. She looked up at me and started to smiling, and blushing. This old ass white woman couldn't have known who the fuck I was, but I was going to use it to my advantage. Most times hospitals wouldn't tell you shit unless you were blood. "Good afternoon, Beautiful. I was wondering if you could tell me what room Leilani Rivera is in?" Lani's dumb ass had told me what floor she was on, but she didn't bother to tell me a room number.

The woman started to rub her neck and look away from me. I had seen that look way too many times. I knew she was thinking about the things she would do to me if she could. I found that older women were always freakier than young broads.

She took a few seconds to gather herself together before she started to bang at her keyboard, one finger at a time. Her eyes were overlooking her glasses as once again she was head first into the monitor. It seemed like she was searching forever. I took out my phone and checked to see if Leilani had texted me, but she didn't.

"She's in the room down the left hallway. 408 will be on your left hand side," she pointed at the direction.

I looked in the direction of the room and nodded my head as I took my hand and started to rub my beard. "Thanks Beautiful, but can you tell me what's going on with her?"

The lady hesitated for a minute and looked around, only to spot a doctor coming our way. "I am so sorry Mr. Kane, but I am not a liberty to say anything. I could lose my job, but that is her doctor. He would know more than I do."

I stood up and waited for the young black man to approach the counter with the clipboard in his hand. He must've noticed that we were about to call her because he addressed the older lady. "What's good Agnus?"

"This young man right here is the husband of Leilani Rivera. He wanted to know about her condition." My head cocked to the side at the word *"husband"*. Now I don't know if Lani's dumb ass told them I was her damn husband or the woman was just assuming, but I'd handle that shit when I saw her.

The doctor looked at me and it was clear that he knew who I was because his entire demeanor changed. He went from being very professional to relaxing his posture like he was one of my boys. "What's good Kane, man. How can I help you?"

He extended his hand out for me to dap him off. It was always funny when I noticed how people would always change with their posture and relax like they were just that cool with me. More men than you would think tried to come at me on a friendly level like I was one of their niggas from their hoods or something.

"What's good Doc. I was wondering if you could tell me how my family is doing? Is the baby ok?" After I dapped him off he, Marri, and I started walking in the direction to the room.

From the way the doctor's face tensed up, the mood was definitely about to change. "Baby? Kane we ran all the tests and there were no indications that Mrs. Rivera is pregnant or that she was recently pregnant." He looked over the folder in his hand and was flipping through the pages.

The anger began to reign through my body from my heart down to my toes, and then back up to my brain. I felt my left eye starting to twitch because this bitch had been lying to me. Causing my life to become more miserable than it already was. This bitch was going to feel my wrath. I was going to make sure that she never sung on a hit song again. Bum ass bitch!

I thanked the doctor for his time and once we got to Lani's room, he and I went our separate ways. I told Marri to wait outside the door because I wouldn't be long. I just didn't want her to see who was in the room and she didn't need to hear my words for her.

The room was dark and very quiet. Wasn't no machines dinging or anything. The TV was on, but it was on mute. The only sounds that were heard was this bitch breathing. My heart was racing because I didn't know how to handle the situation. A part of me wanted to just curse her ass out, but I also wanted her to know how upset I truly was.

Without second guessing it, I wrapped my hand around her throat, squeezing. Her eyes shot open and she started to grab at my hands to get me to move. I loved watching the air escape out of her body. I started to pull her out of the bed by her neck and when her back was all the way off of the bed, I dropped her.

My breathing became heavier and Leilani was shedding tears, holding her neck as she tried to let the oxygen back into her body. "Bitch you lied to me. Talking about you were pregnant. Stupid bitch, I lost my wife from fucking with your wet-back ass. Bitch you'll never work again in this industry. You are done!"

I turned around to walk out of the room, satisfied with what I had told her, but she called out to me to get my attention. As angry as I was, I wanted to know why she would lie like that. "I'm sorry, but I love you so much. I knew that a baby was something that you would become serious about. Even with your initial reaction. Kane, please don't leave me. I love you. I'll kill myself if you leave me."

"That's cool."

# Nineteen

## Emilio

"I need to talk to you about something," I put my fork down and wiped my palms on my jeans. I hadn't thought twice about the conversation I had with Leilani that night, but after what Kelsey told me last night, shit wasn't sitting right with me.

Kelsey shrugged her shoulders while she sprinkled more salt and pepper on to her salad. "Leilani wanted me to kill you. I didn't know it was you she wanted to kill at first, but after you told me that last night, I realized it was you she was talking about."

The reaction Kelsey gave me was just what I was expecting. She just placed her fork down and threw her head into her hands. She was always a silent crier so without seeing her face, I didn't know if she was shedding tears or not.

Although we were in a restaurant, I knew that I needed to comfort her. Kelsey was my one and only real love. Since we were children I loved her and it was stupid of me to even tell her to leave me, but in that moment I didn't want her caught up in the mafia lifestyle. Not everyone was going to be so accepting of her being Black and that scared me, but now I'm a man and I know that I don't need other people's acceptance of my woman. She was my woman.

I got up from my side of the table and slid in the booth on side of Kelsey to console her. Hell I wouldn't know how I would feel either if I randomly found out that my husband's mistress tried to put out a hit on me.

"It's fucking crazy because I didn't do shit to deserve this. I did what I was asked of as a wife and now this shit? First my daughter tells me about my husband cheating, after the bitch been in my face, and now I find out that the bitch wants me dead? Cool."

She lifted her head up to look at me and only a single tear was running down her cheek. I wiped it away with my thumb and pulled her into my chest. "Man fuck him and her. I got you and Kemarr."

That wasn't a lie. I was ready for Kelsey to be in my life for the long haul and now with her being separated from her husband, this was my chance. I knew I was more than twice the man Kane would ever be. Anyone could put together some words and make them rhyme, but it took real skills to run a multimillion dollar casino and resort chain, and even harder skills to run an underground empire.

"So you really want to be with me?" Kelsey scooted away from me, only to stare into my eyes, I guess to make sure I wasn't lying to her. She should know by now that I wouldn't say something I didn't mean.

I pulled her back in and kissed her forehead. "I have never not wanted to be with you. I was just waiting on you to leave that *micio* husband of yours." Hell I been knew her husband was a pussy when he first got into the industry. That nigga wrapped about putting niggas in the ground, but I doubt he'd ever done it.

"Well if you want to be with me, you have to be honest. Are you still in the streets? I don't want random trips to Columbia or Italy. I have a child now and I don't want her around shit like that Milo." Kelsey looked me in the eyes, yet again to make sure I wasn't lying to her, but I was telling the truth. No I wasn't in the streets. I was so high up that niggas came to me. I was the Don.

"No Kelsey, I'm not in the streets. You don't have anything to worry about."

# Twenty

## Kelsey

In the year since I've left King, my life has completely changed. My divorce is final, and Emilio and I decided to get married the very next day. The biggest part of it was finding out that I was pregnant. Kemarr was excited to be a big sister and Emilio was excited about having his first biological child, although his relationship with Kemarr was spectacular.

Life has truly been a dream. King stopped trying to fight me for custody, and I even went back to work. God had truly blessed me.

"So are you going to be working late today," Emilio's voice came through the speaker of my office phone. That was the only thing about Emilio, he hated the fact that I was working. He would rather me be barefoot and pregnant in the kitchen, but that wasn't me. I mean I didn't work as many hours, but now Mr. Michelson had added me to a case involving a kingpin.

I took a deep breath before I responded. "I'll probably be home by seven. Kemarr is going to be by Harmonie since you most likely won't be home."

"Bae, you have been pulling long days all week, and I'm tired of you acting like I can't take care of Kemarr. I'm your husband and her father-figure. I'll pick her up from school." Emilio barked through the phone. I just sat back in my chair and rolled my eyes. It was what the fuck it was.

"Fine Honey. Don't forget she gets out for three." I checked the notification that just came through my phone. It was a text from another lawyer regarding the case. "Babe, I have to go. I have a conference. I love you," I rushed to get my notes together.

"I love you too my Regina." He hung up the phone. I rushed to the conference room where my client and assistant lawyer were waiting with the DA and the assistant DA.

Julius Havok, otherwise known as Big Black, was known in the streets of Atlanta for being ruthless and pushing the most weight, but somehow he got caught up and someone turned him into the police. I was trying my best to get him off, but every time we fight one charge, they find something else to charge him with.

Jonathan Sanders was the DA and he always played hardball as if he had something to prove. Because I mainly defended criminals and celebrities, he and I never really got along. As for him trying to cut one of my clients a deal would only occur in my dreams, so when he said he'd drop Big Black's charges from Kingpin status down to possession, I had to jump on it. The only problem was getting Big Black to talk, but here we were waiting for him to make a full confession.

Everyone in the room looked at me as I entered the room. Being seven months pregnant and trying to slay was taking a toll on me. The five inch heels I wore were slowing me down and I felt as if I was about to fall, but no one would have known by looking at me. Funny thing is before I got with my ex-husband I would have never wore heels. Now I wear them on the daily.

"How nice of it of you to join us Mrs. Taylor or is it Mrs. Gustavo. I just can't seem to keep up with your marital life these days," Sanders started as soon as I sat down next to my client.

He always tried to get under my skin, but I wasn't going to allow him to get me today. "Well Jonathan, you could have a Mrs. as well if your penis wasn't so small." The other's in the room put their heads down and looked away, trying to hold in their laughter. Jonathan rolled his eyes like the little bitch he was. "Now we are here today because my client Mr. Havok has agreed to give a full confession in exchange to having his changes dropped from a Kingpin status to possession with the intentions of distribution."

I looked over at my client and he was sitting in his seat with sweat beads forming on his forehead. He knew what this meant. He was now about to become a snitch. I didn't believe in snitching, but this wasn't about my moral code, but about his life behind bars.

Under my breath, I leaned into his ear to ask him if he was ready. When he informed he was by the nodding of his head, I looked over to the assistant DA who proceeded to start the tape recorder.

Hours had gone by as my client owned up to everything he did which didn't require much of my attention. I sat back in my chair and waited for him to finish. Big Black went over damn near every illegal thing that he'd done. Yet in still, he wasn't done. He had to name those of whom had helped him with these acts.

"Are you ready to name the names?" Sanders sat up in his chair and instructed his assistant to write the names down as well as keep the tape running.

"I was running with different crews. One that I work along with is one from Atlanta. The Boss of that family is Sevyn Matthews. He is responsible for many of the deaths that I took the charges for."

At the mention of that name I damn near choked, but I had to make sure I didn't do anything to draw attention to myself. Sevyn was my best friend's fiancé. I never knew he was in the streets, but now I had to find a way to warn Harmonie without revealing where the fuck I found this out from. I knew it was only a matter of time before the feds were going to go after Sevyn for everything he had.

I watched as Sanders wrote down Sevyn's name and then his assistant did as well. I started to scratch my head out of nervousness. I tried to keep my cool, but now Big Black was seriously talking too much. "He owns several businesses in the area, but his partner owns an even bigger business. I don't know his name, but I do know he is involved with some casino chain. They call him Young Scarface."

This was becoming too much to bare. I felt myself getting more upset as the time went by and I was ready to go. As soon as my client said he was done, I made sure all was squared away and quickly left the conference room.

Once I got my things out of my office, I was ready to go home. I looked at the clock once I got inside of my car and realized it was only ten minutes to six. I'd made good timing, but I couldn't get home fast enough.

I quickly used the Bluetooth in my car to call Harmonie. "Joe's whore house," she answered in her normal childish voice.

There was no way for me to easily tell her what I had to say. "Monie, I need you to meet me tomorrow. For lunch maybe. We need to talk and we need to talk soo."

"Well damn Kels, is it that bad? Can you just say it now? You know I hate waiting." She smacked her lips.

"I'd rather tell you in person. I know how it sounds, but Monie, just meet me at Berreca's for noon," I ordered her. She must've understood the seriousness in my voice because she gave in and agreed to meet me the following afternoon.

After getting off of the phone with her, I felt my baby moving non-stop. It was as if he knew what was going on, but that also meant I needed to calm down. How was one supposed to calm down when I had just heard what I had heard.

Pulling up to the new estate that Emilio and I had recently purchased, I parked right in front of the door. I saw that Emilio's Maybach was further up in the driveway, meaning he was home.

I wasted no time getting out of my vehicle and into the house. Once inside I searched for my husband, but Kemarr's laughter brought me to the kitchen where I found the two of them making pizza.

"Mommy! You are home! Milio picked me up from school and we went got cookies from the place in the mall. Now we are making Pizza. Do you have a special topping you may like?" Kemarr was so happy and I loved seeing her that way. She had flour at the tip of her nose and a little in her hair, which wasn't in the way I had sent her to school.

I went over to her and gave her a kiss on the cheek. Emilio was waiting for his kiss and when he leaned in to kiss me, I turned my head. He leaned back and looked at me, but I rolled my eyes as hard as I possible could. "Kemarr, go wash up please. I'm going to put this pizza in the oven. You did a great job."

The smile I gave her was so fake, but she didn't notice. She wiped her hands on the towel, told Emilio bye, and then hopped off her stool and was out of the kitchen. I waited a few seconds to make sure that she was far enough away before I turned my attention back to my husband.

"Kelsey, what's wrong? I'm not understanding why you are so upset, Is it the hormones?" He wiped his hands on the same towel that Kemarr had just used and then came to try and pull me closer to him.

Pushing him away I walked to the other side of the island to give distance between us because I was too angry to be that close to him. Emilio was still trying to figure out what was wrong, but he allowed the space between us.

"Emilio, what was the only thing I asked of you?" I looked up at the ceiling to try and keep the tears from falling. I caught the ones that formed at the edge of my eyes.

"What are you talking about Bae? I'm confused."

I let out a laugh because I needed to stop myself from crying. He really was so confused and I wasn't understanding how. I haven't asked him for shit since we'd been together. He had to remember my one request. "I fucking asked you to be done with the street life. Didn't I?"

"Yes. I told you I wasn't in the streets. I told you that I haven't been in the streets for a long time," this nigga really lied to my face.

"So they got another Young Scarface out here huh? Another Young Scarface who owns casinos and shit."

Emilio's face went white. He knew he'd been caught and he'd better find a damn good excuse as to why I'm hearing his name in a fucking confessional. "Baby, I can explain. I promise you I can."

I sat down on the stool at the end of the island and folded my arms. I was willing to listen to whatever he had to say, but it had better be good. I had no problem leaving.

Emilio grabbed a glass filled with red wine from the counter and took a sip before he spoke. "You know I would never just lie to you, but I wanted it to be that if something was to happen you could tell the police you didn't know anything and really had been telling the truth."

"I am your fucking wife Emilio!"

"And I know that, but shit is a lot deeper now than when we were first together. I wasn't lying when I said I was in the streets because I wasn't, but I never left the round table. After my father stepped down, I became the boss, or Don,"

I listened to Emilio, but I slowly was feeling let down. He kept all of this shit from me. This man laid next to me every night, keeping secrets. Was anything that he told me the truth? "So you are still in the mob? You are willing to risk my children's life as well as my life and yours? If I don't know, I can't do shit to protect us. Emilio the FEDs are about to be looking for you."

He stared at me waiting to see if I was going to say I was playing, but I wasn't. "How do you know this?" My husband rushed over to my side and got in my face as if the answers were written on my forehead.

"You know I can't say anything. I just warned you," I got up from the stool to put distance between my husband and I again.

Emilio rested with his back against the island and his chin in his hand, thinking. "So you just going to tell me that someone just told you I'm still in the mob and that the FEDs are coming after me, but you can't express to me who? I am your husband Kelsey." His voice remained calm and that was the scariest part because I couldn't pinpoint what would be his next action.

"And I'm your wife, but you will find a way to fix all of this, but until then you'll be sleeping on the couch." I flicked my wrist at him as I left the kitchen and headed towards my room.

"This is my fucking house. I'll sleep where I fucking please." He screamed after me.

"Yea, but it won't be in the bed with me, and put my child's fucking pizza in the oven." I walked up to my room and just fell on to the bed. This shit called life always found a way to throw some shit at me when I think shit is perfect.

# Twenty-One

## Harmonie

I'd been here twenty minutes on my best friend. She was the one who came up with the time we should meet and as always, she was late. I had time to order my food and all, but now I was sitting here nervous as hell trying to figure out what the hell my best friend would have to tell me. My mind went over all different types of scenarios, and all of them were horrible.

"Oh my gosh, I'm sorry I am late. So much is going on. Which is why I needed to speak with you." Kelsey rushed into the restaurant, giving me a kiss on the cheek and taking her seat, placing her Celine bag on the chair next to her.

I gave her a glance over, and I had to admit, she was wearing pregnancy very well. I didn't know if it was because of the new marriage or it was just that pregnancy glow, but it looked darn well on her.

Kelsey called the waiter over to our table and placed her lunch order and her requested a lemonade all before she was ready to start the conversation. The suspense was killing me and it seemed as if she was not in a hurry to spill her tea. "Kelsey, can you tell me why we are here."

"You know you are my best friend, and sister, and I'll always have your best interest at heart," she quickly paused when the waiter came back with her drink. "The case I'm working on now is big shit and you know how Sanders is with any case I take. Well within this case Sevyn's named was mentioned as in being a distributor out here in Atlanta."

As soon as I heard my fiancé's name, I got nervous. I knew what Sevyn did, but he's always assured me that everything would be fine because he had his money laundered. "Are you sure that it was my Sevyn? Sevyn Matthews?"

Kelsey squinted her eyes trying a minute before she answered. "Yes Harmonie, I wouldn't bring this to you if I wasn't more than sure."

I hated lying to my best friend, but like Sevyn said, it wasn't no one's business, but our own. "Well thanks best, but I don't know if that information is accurate. Sevyn runs a nightclub."

Kelsey studied me for a second, but once the food came to the table, her shrimp pasta gained her full attention. I ate my salad quietly, trying not to continue the conversation that we were supposed to be having.

"So how is everything going with my nephew," I'd finally thought of a topic that we both would enjoy discussing. "I know Milo is over joyed."

Kelsey looked up from her food, and shrugged her shoulders. "He's good. Ready to come out, but other than that, everything is good." Her voice was dry and I knew she felt some type of way by the way I reacted to the information she'd given me, but she'd just have to get over it.

After lunch with Kelsey, I headed back home because I was feeling uneasy. I knew once I brought this shit to Sevyn, he'd be beyond upset and I wasn't ready to deal with it. Thankfully for me he wasn't home when I got there.

I entered the townhome that we would be staying in until the after the wedding, and I felt the sense of loneliness that filled the house. Sevyn was always gone, but even when he was here, his mind was somewhere else.

My relationship with Sevyn was what I would consider to be complicated. I knew he loved me, but his ways just always kept us from fully being together. It was as if nothing I did was good enough from him, and the sad part was, I couldn't tell my best friend anything. Yea, Kelsey would've been there for me, but at the same time she probably wouldn't understand the half of it.

Since I was home alone I spent the evening looking over the statements for my clients. One thing I could say about Sevyn is that he brought me a lot of business. Many of his business partners in the game decided to trust me with their coins and I've been making sure that the FED's wouldn't suspect anything out of the ordinary.

Just nine that night, Sevyn walked through the doors of the of my office, drunk and angry. As soon as I saw him coming my way, I dashed from behind my desk. Running out of the office, I started to run up the stairs, but Sevyn caught be by my left ankle and pulled me back down.

"What is this shit I'm hearing in the streets that your best friend's client is out there giving my name to the DA huh? What the fuck did you tell her?" I felt his fist collide with my jaw and I felt myself start to choke on the blood.

Trying to fight him off was to no prevail because Sevyn was at least eighty pounds heavier than I was. "I told you about having her ass in our fucking business."

"I didn't tell her anything, I promise. She just told today, and I lied to her. Sevyn please." I couldn't fight back anymore so I just blocked his punches. He must have worn himself out because he sat next to me on the stairs and wiped the sweat from his forehead before he pulled me closer to him.

This was a normal Tuesday in the life of Sevyn and Harmonie. Fight after fight and just like a fool, I stayed. It wasn't just Sevyn that started fights though, I had my fair share too; maybe not as much as my fiancé, but enough.

"Babe, I promise you that I didn't tell Kelsey anything. You have to believe me," I sobbed into his chest. Sevyn started to rub my back, but he didn't say anything. "Do you believe me? Tell me that you believe me."

I reached up to grab his face, but he wouldn't look at me. I planted small kisses on his lips until he responded to me. "You want me to believe you?" I nodded my head as fast as I could. "Call the police and turn Emilio Gustavo in."

I shook my head because I knew he couldn't be serious. How could he expect me to turn in my best friend's husband? Especially with her being pregnant with his child. Sevyn stood up and laughed me off. "You choosing that nigga over me?"

"No, but he's Kelsey's husband and her child's father." I exclaimed to him, but he wasn't buying it. He looked down at me and shook his head with his hands on his hips.

"If you want me to believe you, I told you what the fuck you had to do, point blank."

# Twenty-Two

## King

"Man you dumb as hell. You lost your wife and now your house looks like shit. Did the maids divorce your ass too?" Chantae walked around my house with her hands on her hips, looking around my house in disappointment.

"We didn't have no fucking maids, I snapped at her." I threw my leg up on the couch and popped open my beer. Since this damn divorce this has been my life if I wasn't in the studio or with my daughter.

Tae sat down on the sofa with me before she responded. "You mean to tell me that Kelsey took care of this big ass house by her damn self? How many rooms y'all got? Six?"

"Seven," I shrugged my shoulders and looked for the remote without moving my back from against the sofa.

Tae she laughed at my situation, but I didn't see shit funny. Hell it still wasn't real to me that my wife had married someone else and was having a baby by the bitch nigga. All because I fucked another bitch, talk about childish.

I did get some satisfaction with making sure Leilani's career was over before it really got started. After making sure to talking to our record label, I made sure that she wasn't about to be in nobody's top ten no time soon. She hasn't spoken to me since, but that was cool with me too. There had been a different bitch in my bed every night since my divorce.

I sat and watched TV with Tae for about an hour before it was time for me to head to the studio and help one of the artists that my label had recently signed. Although they had offered me to start signing to my own artists, but that wasn't what I wanted to do right now. I wasn't ready for the responsibility right now.

The studio was lit and they had muth'fuckas all around. Niggas who clearly had no purpose there, but to sit, smoke, and drink. "Nah son, all these extra people in the studio not gon work. You will lose focus. If you aren't signed to a fucking label, get out!" I held the door open. The lame niggas looked at Nymph as if he was going to go against me, but he just shrugged his shoulders.

Slowly the studio started to empty out leaving just Nymph, Dee, and myself. I was gonna have Johnny stop by later, but that was different. He had an ear for good music and he was a recruiter for the label, so he wasn't no lych.

"Say Nymph, you keep all them niggas on your payroll for nothing, that's the quickest way to become broke. I'm not saying that you have to forget where you came from, but manage your money my nigga." I dapped Nymph and Dee off and gave him a piece of advice. I have seen so many niggas come in this industry sign a big deal and just go broke spending the money carelessly.

Nymph agreed with me by shaking his head. "Yea, niggas be wanting to eat, but not put in the work," Dee added his two cents.

"Yea, but say let's get this work done. I got shit to do." I set down at the board and waited for Nymph to get up and go in the booth.

He was a hot up and coming rapper, and I felt like he could become a heavy hitter in the game. His rhymes were raw and he actually went through what he rapped about. He was from the streets, and had been on his own since he was seven. I don't know how he managed to stay out of foster care and shit, but he raised himself.

It didn't take long for Nymph to drop his verse for his tack, so the rest of the time we started to discuss the plans for him to release a mixtape while his fans waited on the album. Today, artists needed to always make sure that they always kept something for their fans to listen to because if not, someone else could drop something to make the fans lose focus.

A buzz through the intercom interrupted our focus. I figured that it was Johnny so I just hit the button to let him in, I was actually glad he was stopping by. Since the divorce, he and I were in the streets like we were kids.

When the door opened to the studio, I felt the steam come through my ears. "Bitch, what the fuck are you doing here?" I rose out of my chair and charged at Leilani. Her eyes protruded from her head as I cornered her in.

It didn't matter that two other men were in the room; I was going to let this bitch have it. She knew better than to ever be in my presence again after what had gone down between us. "Kane, please just talk to me. I need you. They are about to foreclose on my house, please Baby."

Leilani extended her arms to try and convince me with her hands, but I backed away from her and glared at her. I knew damn well this bitch didn't come down here to beg. She had better luck getting the damn devil to help her than she had getting me.

The tears started to form in the ducts of her eyes and she started shaking and then scratching. "Bitch are you on something?" I studied her more to see what was going on, but she was scratching rubbing the back of her nap. As mad as I was at her, she was too pretty to be some somebody's narcotic.

"Just leave Lani. Just gon head and go bruh before you piss me the fuck off. I can't believe your stupid ass is on some fucking drugs." I backed away from her and nodded my heads towards the door, but she still didn't move. "NOW," I used the bass in my voice to scare her a little bit. She rushed out of the studio like a roach when the light came on.

When I turned around Dee and Nymph were staring at me. "What the fuck y'all lookin at huh? That's what happen when you piss me the fuck off."

# Twenty-Three

## Kelsey

With my husband's freedom being on the line, I was working even the harder to get Big Black off. I was trying to find as many faults in the state's case and so far, they had everything on lock. I was either going to have to sabotage it legally or illegally, but either way my man wasn't going to jail.

I had even been trying to handle some stuff for Sevyn, but since Harmonie hadn't been answering my calls for the past week, nor did she answer the door when I stopped by the house, I had no information on him besides knowing he owned a club, so there really wasn't much I could defend him on.

No one was aware yet who Young Scarface was, so there was no need for me to resign from the case. As far as I was concerned, I was going to play dumb when they confronted me about it.

Just as I was preparing my final notes to the new information I had received that day, Sharmane paged into my office. "Kels, your husband is here," her cheerful voice came through the speaker.

Chills ran through my body because I didn't want my husband to see the facts that I had on the case. That could cause me to lose my license as a practicing attorney. I pressed to button to respond to her as I closed the folder to the documents. "Send him in, please." Sharmane said he was already on his way back, and he made good time because just as the door to my office was opening, I had cleared my desk off.

I locked eyes with my fine ass husband and licked my lips. Today was wasn't in his usual suit and tie. He had on a bomber jacket, a pair of dark grey tight fitting jeans, a loose white V-neck, and some all-white Adidas; my man was fine. "Ciao mi Regina," his thick Italian accent led his way into the room.

"Hey Husband, what brings you by?" I leaned forward in my chair, resting my elbows on my desk. Milo walked over to my desk and bent down to taste my lips. Damn, this man even spelled good. If I wasn't married to him, I would just have to marry him.

"I came to take my beautiful wife out for the day. I know that things have been hard with everything being out in the open, but you my baby." He sat down in the chair in front of my desk and rested, with his legs open. Although his jeans were not super skinny, they were just tight enough for me to slightly see his package resting on his right thigh.

Pregnancy had made me extremely horny and heaven knew that my husband always scratched my itch. Emilio must have noticed me looking at him because he licked his lips and then said, "You lookin real good. Stand up and let Daddy see." Following his command, I stood up, revealing the tight maroon cotton dress with a scoop neckline. The black string-up heels complemented it just fine.

Milo used his finger and called me over to him. I did a little spin right in front of his face and stopped once my ass faced him. It had gotten plumper with this pregnancy too. Emilio leaned forward and kissed it. I felt his hands come under my dress and started to rub my thighs. His touch made me melt, and the feeling I felt in my toes when his fingers slid under my panties and touched my second set of lips, was everything.

Emilio stood up behind me, retrieving his hands, only to lead me over to my desk. Thankfully I had cleared it off, so My husband laid me on my back, next to my Apple computer. My legs hung over the edge and I watched as he slowly removed my panties and threw them to the chair that he was recently sitting.

Once he got on his knees, I knew what was to come. The tip of his tongue ran along my slit and kindly touched my clit. I felt a cooling sensation sprung through my body and relaxed my muscles, allowing my husband to pleasure me. He frenched my pearl and then inserted a finger, causing me to exude my juices.

After achieving an orgasm, my husband stood up and reintroduced me to his thick, long, member. Pushing inside of me, my reflexes causes me to arch my back. Emilio started to slowly work up a rhythm, giving me slow, deep strokes. Wrapping my legs around his neck, I used my hands and started to massage my breasts. Closing my eyes only heightened the experience. I felt everything he was doing to my body, and I loved it.

Moans were escaping out of my mouth with each thrust, and as low as I tried to keep them, some were high pitched. "You like that shit huh?" His spoke in between groans, but I couldn't answer him because my body was taken over by an orgasm. "Huh Kelsey, you like that shit?" Emilio's voice got deeper as he sped up his strokes, placing his hand on the nape of my neck.

"Yes, yes. I like it." I spoke through my teeth because I was having yet another orgasm. Emilio was tearing my shit up and I felt his dick in my heart. "I can't take this baby, I can't."

Instead of him slowing down or stopping altogether, he sped up his pace even more. "No baby, take it. Hold off for me." He moved his hand from my neck and grabbed a hold of my waist. Soon, he released himself inside of me and I felt the warm liquid coat my walls, causing me to cum once again.

Emilio pulled himself from inside of me and fell back into the chair to catch his breath. I laid still on the desk and tried my hardest to keep to regain my strength, but I keep feeling my clit throbbing and my actual vagina pulsate. Gosh, what was this man doing to me?

"Get up, let's go get lunch."

# Twenty-Four

## Emilio

"So I was thinking about the name Giovanni," Kelsey sat suggested as we sat on the park bench watching Kemarr play on the playset. Although it was a bit chilly outside, it felt nice just to be with my family.

"I like it. I wanted another Emilio, but Giovanni is what we will go with. Giovanni Emilio Gustavo." The name sounded like a real Don to me, and I liked it. I wanted my child's name to have power, something strong.

Kelsey kissed me on he cheek, pleased at the fact that I liked her name. We had been looking for names the entire eight months she had been pregnant and this was the first one that I liked.

My wife didn't know the real reason why I wanted to spend time with her and Kemarr today, but that wasn't for her to know. It'd gotten back to me that the FED's were closing in on me and it was only a matter of time before the called me. Soon she would be getting a call that Big Black had been killed in a prison yard fight, but I didn't know how long I had as a free man. I was hoping that my lawyers could work something out and get me off. I knew that getting indicted in the south was my biggest mistake, but I was hoping that someone in my family had a connection with a political figure somewhere in Georgia, but if not I was facing life behind bars.

Until all that shit happened, I decided that I was going to lie low and get in as much time with my wife, step-child, and unborn as I could. I'd gotten rid of everything and was allowing my nephew to temporarily run the cartel until this shit got settled.

"You know, no matter what the outcome is with this Big Black case, I'm going to stand by you. You are my soulmate, and I love you. God is going to work something out, I believe it." Kelsey's words were like she was reading my mind. It was shit like that about her that made me crazy about her. She knew what I was thinking before I said it, and half the time she would finish my sentences.

I acknowledged her words by kissing her on her forehead. Being emotional wasn't in my DNA, but somehow I was now getting a little hot in all of this cold. "Don't stress it bae. You're pregnant." I patted her thigh. "Kemarr, want us to come play with you?"

Kemarr was in the middle of playing a game of it with the other kids on the playground, but as soon as I asked, she ran over to us and stood in front of Kelsey and I, tucking one of her three long braids behind her ear. "Can one of y'all push me?"

"Yea I'll push you, come on." I stood up from the bench and followed her over to the swing sets. There were only three swings, which were all full, and a line of six people waiting.

"Manny, I'm not waiting for all these people to have a turn. Can we go to Chuck-E-Cheese or something?" Kemarr shook her head at the line and then stopped in her tracks to turn and asked me to leave.

Hell the child had sense because there wasn't a way in hell I was going to wait for a turn on the swing. "Yea, let's go. Chuck-E-Cheese it is."

"Cool, Manny. Let me go tell my momma," she ran off ahead of me. Manny was what Kemarr had been calling me since Kelsey and I got married. She said that she already had a daddy and since my name was Milo, I would be her Manny since Manny rhymed with Daddy. I couldn't argue with the child because the shit made sense. I always told Kelsey that her child had lived before.

Being it a random weekday afternoon, Chuck-E-Cheese was pretty quiet, which Kemarr didn't mind because that meant she could hop from machine to machine without having to wait. Kelsey was happy too with the pizza and wings that I'd ordered. She sat at the table, eating, while Kemarr and I played the games.

"You are pretty good with your daughter," a lady standing next to me by the skee-ball machine. I'd spotted her earlier checking me out as she watched her son run around this damn place like a jackrabbit.

I nodded my head and thanked her. She flashed me a smile, and she was pretty chocolate girl, but I wasn't trying to fuck up my marriage. My days of cheating were long over. I continued to play with Kemarr on the machine. Her cheating ass climbed on top and started throwing the balls in herself.

"Y'all come out here often? If so, we should hook up sometimes. I'm always looking for my son to have someone to play with." The lady got even closer. I can't lie she was making me a bit uncomfortable because I wasn't for a woman to be so upfront.

"Nah, my husband has all the hooking up her can handle," I heard Kelsey's voice as I felt her body rub against mine. I looked over my shoulder and my wife was standing right behind me with the pettiest smile ever. The lady must've gotten the hint because she kissed her teeth and grabbed her son's hand, moving him away from us.

Kelsey came in front of me and wrapped her arms around my waist. "Get these bitches in here hurt Emilio." I laughed it off, but I knew she was serious. "Don't try me," she rolled her eyes and moved away from me, going to play with Kemarr, who had moved down to another game.

We had to be in the place for about two hours just having a good time. Kemarr so many tickets that the machines started to run out, but she still wasn't done. "Kemarr, you have five more tokens and then it is time to go home," Kelsey spoke in a stern voice.

Kemarr's look of aggravation was hilarious, but her mother was about to slice her throat when she heard her mumble something. "We can go now if it's a problem."

"Babe, let her have fun. Come with me to the table," I implored, while trying to contain my laughter. Once she gave in, we went back to the table. I wanted finally tell her what was going on. I didn't want her to be in the dark.

As soon as Kelsey sat down, she picked up a slice of pizza. She didn't even bother to ask me if I wanted the last wing because she ate that too. She had three more weeks to be pregnant and, I was ready for it to be over. There was no sharing or anything. It was simply *Kelsey wants so Kelsey eats*.

After she washed down her food with my water, I figured it was time for me to tell her. "I need to talk to you about something," I bit my bottom lip.

Before I got the chance to finish my sentence, a swarm of FED's surrounded our table. It felt like a dream because this shit could not be happening. This shit was happening to soon, how did they even know I was here?

"What the fuck is going on," Kelsey looked puzzled as the men pulled me from my chair. I didn't put up a fight because I knew what was happening. "Emilio, wait." She stood up and started to try and pull the officers away from me.

In retaliation, they started pushing her back, clearly ignoring her bulging belly. That was when the anger set in. "She is pregnant, let her be," I screamed.

"Emilio Gustavo you are under arrest for the distribution of illegal narcotics, money laundering, and murder," one tall Black cop started to read me my rights. Kelsey still was arguing are screaming for them to let me go. My head started to get foggy when I heard Kemarr's voice calling my name and begging the officers to let me go.

They ignored all of their cries and started shoving me towards to the doors of the establishment. My chest started to go up and down as anger filled my heart. This was not how this was supposed to go down. I knew that eventually they were going to arrest me, but I never wanted it to be in the presence of my family.

"Oh my gosh," I heard my wife's voice. She wasn't screaming or crying, but she sounded shocked which was caused me to stop walking and look back. When I looked back, Kelsey was in the middle of the aisle holding her stomach.

"Ma, you peed on yourself," Kemarr asked still crying, but Kelsey shook her head. She looked me in my eyes and I could see the pain in her soul.

"My water just broke."

# Twenty-Five

## Kelsey

My three-hour labor wasn't painful because I pushed a baby out of me, but because I had to go through it alone. My husband was in prison; my best friend wasn't talking to me; so all I had was Kemarr to coach me through.

I cried nonstop as I pushed Giovanni out. I cried as the laid him on my chest for the first skin-to-skin moments. I cried when the nurse asked me what we would call him. I cried when the nurse had to pick Kemarr up to cut the umbilical cord. I cried even harder when the same nurse asked me if Kemarr could go with her to help with Giovanni's bath since his father wasn't present. For six straight hours, I cried.

It was as if I couldn't win for losing in this game called life. There was no reason why my husband had to be taken from me so soon. All I wanted was a fucking happy ending, and I couldn't even get that.

After being in the hospital for so long, I decided to call someone and let them know where I was so they could come and take Kemarr home or at least to get some changing clothes. Sharmane answered me on the first ring and was here within an hour. She'd stopped by my home to get clothes for Kemarr and things for me. She even brought food for us. My mother had vowed to be on the next plane to Atlanta, and of course Harmonie didn't answer me.

As upset as I was, I didn't have time to think about it because the nurse had brought Giovanni back in the room to be fed. With the frustration of everything else going on, the last thing I needed was for my son not to latch to my nipple right away. He refused to feed from me and every time I tried, he screamed.

"Babies can tell when their mothers are stressed, so that may cause them not to feed," she tried to calm me, but that only stressed me out even more. Tears escaped from my eyes, and I held my child in my lap and felt sorry. Here I was about to have another child without the daddy being there like a father should. Sharmane tried to come and rub my back, but that only made it worse. So eventually the nurse took my child from me and asked me to pump my milk and she would feed him for me.

It was the same pattern for the next two days. My mom arrived in town and she took care of Kemarr and when she came to the hospital, she took care of Giovanni. I laid in bed, and didn't move. I didn't eat or drink anything. I was hopeless, and although I didn't want to feel like this, I couldn't help it. Especially since in two days I haven't heard from my husband, and Sharmane couldn't track him to jail.

"Look you have a visitor," my nurse walked in all cheery, carrying a bouquet of flowers. My room was decorated in all kinds of congratulatory items from family since my mother got on the phone and ran her mouth to everyone she thought about.

I didn't bother to look at who the visitor was following my nurse because I really didn't care, but once the person spoke I knew who it was and my blood began to boil as the hatred filled my body. "Hello," Leilani's soft spoken voice intruded my ear canals.

I waited for the nurse to leave so I could beat the bitch's ass. I was ready to beat her worse than I had in the club. I withdrew the covers from my body and got out the bed, flying towards her. As soon as I got close enough I wrapped my hands in her hair. "Wait, let me explain! No one is who you think they are!"

For some odd reason, I chose to let he explain, but not before throwing her into the wall. "Talk bitch or swear I'm gonna shove my foot so far up your ass you will be spitting out yellow nail polish for a week," I rolled my eyes and made my way back to the hospital bed. I had worn myself out trying to get revenge.

Leilani didn't get up from the floor, but fixed her hair before she started to talk. The bitch was scratching too; probably on some drug. "Your best friend ain't who you believe she is." I watched her dig in her purse and pull out a sheet of paper.

"What are you talking about?" This bitch didn't even know my best friend and now she was going to tell me I didn't know her.

Finally, Leilani stood up and walked to my bed and handed me the folded piece of paper. Opening, I didn't know what I was looking at, but I saw that it was from the Women's Center of New Jersey. "Five years ago Harmonie had an abortion," Leilani started her speech all over again.

She was starting to irk my soul now. Bitch wasn't getting to the point. What the fuck my best friend having an abortion got to do with me? Wasn't my ass killing children. "Leilani, I swear before The Lord, you got three seconds to,"

Before I could finish threatening the inane broad, she cut me off. "Look who the card was registered to. Look at who paid for it," she came stood over my shoulders.

My eyes scattered across the paper, now my hands were shaking because I didn't know what I was about to find out. Who paid for it, but when I saw it, my heart sunk. Emilio Gustavo was typed clear as day next to Master Card and the last four of his card number. That had to mean Emilio was the father, but how why? Both of them knew my relationship with the other, and yet they still messed around behind my back.

"That isn't everything. I know who turned your husband in," she started to scratch again. I waited for her to finish her statement. "It was Sevyn, he got Harmonie to do it."

Blow after blow Leilani came in and further kicked my sorrows closer to hell. Leilani was right, I didn't know my best friend at all. Everything was a lie. Hell how had Leilani come back into my life and still manage to fuck shit up.

After a while of not saying anything, Leilani gathered her things and began to head out of the door. "Wait," I shouted after her. She turned around and looked at me, waiting for me to talk. "How do you know all of this?"

Leilani hung her head and then looked at the ceiling and shook her head. "Because I'm sleeping with Sevyn,"

I laughed at the irony. She slept with my husband and now she was sleeping with Harmonie's fiancé. I motioned for her to leave the room because I was officially done with everything. At this point, I was sure nothing else could go wrong, but I probably spoke too soon.

My phone started to light up on the tv-tray and looked down and saw my mother's name. "Hello," I spoke dryly not really wanting to talk.

"Kelsey, the FEDs are at your house baby."